M.M KUSHI

Survivor

Copyright © 2023 by M.M Kushi

All rights reserved. No part of this publication may be reproduced, stored or transmitted in any form or by any means, electronic, mechanical, photocopying, recording, scanning, or otherwise without written permission from the publisher. It is illegal to copy this book, post it to a website, or distribute it by any other means without permission.

First edition

This book was professionally typeset on Reedsy. Find out more at reedsy.com

For all of the Maras

Foreword

Survivor contains scenes that may be disturbing to some readers including depictions of abuse, death, violence, suicidal thoughts, and rape. Please read with care.

1

My fingers brushed the velvety petals of the pale pink blossom. Pink had been my mother's favorite color.

Sorrow crept into me, and I drew a deep breath before letting the flower fall. Leaves rustled in the cool evening breeze and I sighed at the memories that tried to force themselves to the forefront of my consciousness. My mother's face hovered there, her blonde hair slicked back into her signature bun, the corners of her full lips turned up in a wide grin as she flashed her pretty white teeth.

Her laugh rang like church bells through my mind, bounding around in the shadows and coaxing more memories out. She was so vivid I could almost reach out and touch her, almost feel her warmth under my fingertips. I tried to will myself forward, but I remained rooted in place. As I stood there and stared at her, the scene twisted into something darker. Her face contorted, her eyebrows knitting together, her eyes crinkling in the corners as she winced. Her lips formed a shocked little 'O' before opening wide. An ear-piercing scream burst from her.

I stumbled back, clamping my hand over my mouth to muffle the shocked squeal as the heel of my boot thumped into a root and I tumbled onto the ground. I was faintly aware of the dull pain radiating up my back, but the edges of my vision grew blurry as I focused in on the blood blossoming across my mother's pale yellow dress and dripping from the hem onto the grass.

I knew that scream.

I clamped my hands over my ears, trying desperately to drown it out, squeezing my eyes shut. Her cries grew higher and I curled into myself, tucking my knees to my chest. A sickening gurgle replaced the sounds and my chest tightened, crushing my lungs until I thought I might suffocate.

"Help." Her voice was weak as she pleaded. I knew it was too late for her and I squeezed my eyes shut even tighter. *Coward. You're a coward.* The tears came faster now, but I bit my tongue to hold back the choking sobs. My mind searched desperately for anything to latch onto to justify what my body had done. My parents loved me, they told me so a thousand times. They would have wanted me to live, to have a fighting chance at life. I clutched at that thought like a life preserver, desperate to save myself from drowning in the guilt of my actions. *I'm sorry. I'm so sorry.* I was going to be given a one-way ticket to hell when I died... I deserved it.

"I wish I could take it back." My voice startled me and I flinched, my eyes popping open to find my mother gone. The weight pressing down on me began to lighten and I gasped for the air I had been starved of. The trees swayed lazily in the breeze, their branches twisting and turning softly. The grass was soft against my bare legs and I ran my fingers through the lush blades.

Real.

The air stung as it filled my aching lungs repeatedly, my head swimming as I could finally relax. The sky had gone dark, how long ago I couldn't be sure. Stars glittered overhead, like white paint splattered across a midnight canvas. The others would be worried by now; I had only meant to be gone long enough to search for a few edible plants. That had to have been hours ago. I could almost hear Lucy's unforgiving voice lecturing me about the importance of never staying out past dark by myself. *It's not safe in the darkness, Sophia.*

Monsters hid in the dark, creeping along in the shadows where you couldn't see them, preying on the unfortunate souls that didn't hear them coming. The night sounds had already started. The chirping of crickets and the soft rustling of rodents, as they scurried through the long dead leaves, were a comforting reminder that I was not truly alone... that nothing more dangerous was lurking in the shadows between the trees.

I drew a shaky breath, pushing my sweat-drenched hair back from my face as I got to my feet. I sighed and began picking my way through the thick underbrush toward camp. I lost my footing in the darkness a few times, tripping over tree roots hidden in the long dry bed of pine needles. My palms burned as I slammed them into the rough bark of the surrounding trees, trying to stay upright as I staggered blindly in the direction I remembered coming from. It wasn't a long trek back, though it was longer than it had been in the daylight. The darkness made everything seem longer. The glow of the once roaring fire had died to only embers by the time I stumbled into the small clearing— no doubt thanks to an overly cautious Mason insisting that the flames be smothered after the sun began to sink below the treetops.

"Where were you?" Lucy's voice bit into me. I cringed inwardly as I turned to look at her. Her arms were crossed, her brows pulled down as she scowled at me.

"I lost track of time." I knew it sounded like a lie when I said it, and she never believed my lies.

She snorted her disapproval. "I'm sure you did."

I hunched my shoulders and hurried over to my designated sleep space, crawling into the sleeping bag and curling into a ball. Beside me, Jax snored softly, the rise and fall of her form a familiar comfort. I'm not sure how long I laid in the darkness, unable to sleep... too afraid of the memories that would assault me in my dreams. Finally, I sat up with an irritated huff and looked around the camp. Beside me, Jax was curled into a tight ball, the blanket thrown over her head so only the ends of her chestnut hair peeked out from beneath the fleece fabric. On the other side of her, Mason's deep breaths hummed in a steady rhythm, his large frame buried deep in the layers of blankets. He was folded carefully into the small space, somehow making a home out of something he did not quite fit into.

I flopped over and found Lucy's sleeping bag empty. *Why does she even bother rolling it out?* I stared silently at the dark wrinkled fabric for a few beats before I quietly slipped out and slid my boots on. I scanned the clearing and almost missed her small frame, hidden in the murky shadows of the trees, bathed in the darkness. I crept towards her slowly, ensuring that my boot came down on the long dead leaves and sporadically littered branches so I didn't startle her. She looked like a predator lurking in the trees, her muscular body wound tightly.

"What do you want?" She didn't turn her head.

I froze. "Why didn't you get me to change shifts?"

"I figured you needed the sleep." She did this way more often than I was comfortable with, letting herself stay awake for days on end in the name of my sleep.

"I think you're lying." The words were past my lips before I could stop them and I quickly snapped my mouth shut. It was dangerous to provoke her, like poking a sleeping bear.

"Think what you want, Soph." She turned to look at me, her form silhouetted in the icy moonlight. The scars decorating her face glimmered in the darkness, the smooth skin stretched tightly across her tan skin, distorting her features on one side.

"You need sleep too," I finally whispered, part of me praying that she wouldn't hear me.

"I'm alright." Her tone was matter-of-fact, and she leaned back against the trunk of the tree, crossing her arms.

I stood quietly as I drew a deep breath, filling my lungs to the brim with the humid night air, contemplating whether it was worth it to fight with her. "You can't stay awake forever," I finally managed.

"I said I'm alright, Sophia." Her words were a sharp-edged blade pressed against my skin, daring me to keep pushing her. Sometimes I would take the bait and push her to the point of breaking, but tonight would not be one of those nights. She turned away from me again, angling herself so her back was mostly to me. She always wanted me to leave her alone these days. *Just go.*

I huffed but walked back to my sleeping bag, sinking to the ground and pulling my knees to my chest. Sleep wasn't in the cards tonight. Around us, the night was alive with the chorus of life. The comforting sound of animals scurrying through the underbrush and the gust of wind beneath an owl's wings lulled me into a false sense of security. Sometimes, I could almost pretend that everything was normal… that the world wasn't falling to pieces

1

around us. Then the crack of something heavy would join the quiet, familiar hum and ice would race through my veins. There was nothing normal about this life anymore.

I used to devour stories about the apocalypse, hungry for the monsters they contained. Zombies were always my favorite. Something about the idea that death wasn't always final thrilled me. Much of my early teen years were spent with my nose buried in book after book, comparing different types of zombies and thinking I knew everything and would be ready when the world truly ended. A lot of people thought that they were ready. Entire events were dedicated to "surviving the apocalypse". We thought they were fun, disillusioned into the belief that surviving a simulated end of the world was enough to prove us worthy of survival when the real end came. But those were just pretend. Nothing could have prepared the world for the hell on Earth that the apocalypse would bring. The medals and ribbons that had hung on my bedroom wall announcing me a survivor meant nothing when the real monsters came calling.

Lucy called them shredders, partly because we had no other name for them, but mostly because of the gruesome things they did. We spent our apocalypse running, hiding like rats in the sewer, hoping that maybe we'd wake up and it would have all been a dream. Or maybe someone would yell 'cut' and the chaos would have all simply been movie magic.

I rested my chin on my knees, staring into the darkness of the surrounding trees, terrified of what might be lurking just beyond. Being afraid of the dark took on a whole new meaning now, but we were never really afraid of the dark, were we? We were afraid of the things that hunted in the dark, that used the shadows to conceal themselves from us.

Everyone had their theories about how everything started and why. They ranged from divine punishment to science experiments gone wrong to population control. I listened to them all, but ultimately decided that I didn't care how or why it started, I only cared that I had been foolish enough to wish for it.

Even when it first started, I was a stupid 16-year-old who was excited to live like the characters in my favorite stories. I remembered the way my heart jumped at the thought of getting the chance to prove that I was a survivor, that I was one of the few that would make it. That was when there were only a few of them and the military said it wasn't anything to be worried about. Then the government said that everything was under control. We should have known better.

2

Sunlight washed over my face and pulled me from my foggy stupor. Sleep never came, but my mind had drifted deep into itself. I groggily looked around and found Lucy still perched on the trunk of a fallen tree not far from us. She looked like she hadn't moved all night. *Why does she torture herself?* Jax and Mason were still sound asleep, their soft breathing and quiet snores familiar and comforting. Jax's head was still buried under her blanket, the tail of her stuffed whale sticking out, and I smiled to myself as I stared at her.

Shades of pink and blue exploded across the sky as the sun crested the horizon and lazily floated upward. I stretched out my legs and yawned before getting to my feet, my joints and muscles hissing at me as I went.

"I'm going to go look for some food," I announced, flinging my bag over my shoulder and heading toward the trees.

"Don't lose track of time again, Sophia!" Lucy called after me, the threat heavy in her voice. I raised a hand sheepishly before allowing the trees to swallow me. Dew clung to the leaves and blades of grass, the droplets sticking in my hair and washing across my face as I moved deeper into the forest. Blackberry bushes grew abundantly in this area and I found dozens of them over the last few weeks. The sun hadn't risen enough to light up the deepest parts of the forest yet, and I stumbled through the shadows, tripping over hidden roots and snagging my shirt on outstretched branches. At least the bears would know that I was coming and hopefully move off.

The sun had almost reached the center of the sky by the time I happened upon a small patch of bushes that hadn't been picked clean by wildlife. I hurriedly filled my bag with the ripe berries, their dark purple juice staining my fingers as I ripped them free from the thorned branches. The jagged spikes scraped at my skin and I prayed that they didn't draw blood. Berries still sat deeper in the bushes, taunting me, but the thorns bred overwhelming fear that settled heavily in my stomach.

With a heavy sigh, I headed back in the direction of camp, hoping the berries would be enough to last until tomorrow. The snap of a branch startled me, my heart rate picking up as fear laced itself through me. I turned in a slow circle, my muscles tense in an attempt to remain quiet. I scanned the trees, a silent prayer poised on the tip of my tongue. The snap came again. I blinked rapidly to keep the tears from falling.

"Please." The plea was nothing more than a faint whisper, the last bit of my hope escaping. More snaps turned my blood to ice in my veins and I could no longer keep the tears at bay. My breath hitched in my throat. *This is it. This is where it all ends.* My heart pounded frantically against my ribs, threatening to explode with each beat. The leaves rustled and another snap came from my left. I wanted to close my eyes but fear kept them wide open; I needed to see death coming for me. The leaves rustled again, and a strangled sob fell from my lips. A deer leaped from the shadow of the trees, staring at me only for a moment before rushing off. I reached to clutch at my chest, willing my heart to slow down, to hopefully return to a normal pace. Once my breathing had slowed I continued toward camp. *You'll die of a heart attack if you aren't careful.*

"Sophia!" My name echoed playfully around me as I stepped back into the clearing and I smirked. Jax bounded up to me like a lost puppy, her face flushed from the sun and thick humidity. The spattering of freckles across her cheeks had grown more prominent over the months and had multiplied as the days passed. A stray curl escaped the tight bun she always wore and she brushed it from her eyes with an irritated huff.

"Did I miss anything?" I asked, slipping the bag from my shoulders. It fell to the ground at my feet with a soft thump, stirring up a small cloud of dust.

"Mason shot a rabbit," she pouted, her forehead wrinkling as she glared at the ground. I sometimes forgot she was a child, but times like this made me remember the scared little girl that Lucy and I found cowering behind a dumpster on our way out of the city. She couldn't have been older than eight or nine then, though we weren't sure since she refused to tell us anything more than her name.

"And because of Mason, you have food," I cooed, reaching down and dumping the berries out onto my sleeping bag. I frowned down at the pile, painfully aware of how few berries there were now that I saw them all laid out.

She plopped down in front of the berries and began picking the leaves and twigs out of the pile. "I still don't see why the berries aren't enough."

From this angle, I could see her bottom lip jut out like a toddler and I chuckled to myself before answering, "The berry bushes are getting few and far between Jax. There aren't enough of them. These won't even last until tomorrow."

"I just don't like hurting things," she mumbled.

"It's what we have to do to survive, Jax." Lucy's voice was gentle when she spoke, walking from the far side of the camp. "Survival isn't always pretty." She pushed her hair back from her face, her sweat holding the short, choppy strands smooth against her head. The largest of her scars stretched from the corner of her lips up past her eyebrow and disappeared into her hairline. I remembered the barbed wire that had caused that scar, the look of panic on her face as the blood poured down her cheek and pooled on the ground, and her scream of agony as I pressed a hot piece of metal against the cut to cauterize it and stop the bleeding. I spent weeks after that fearing that I would lose her to an infection, but she was a fighter. The other scars were much smaller, by comparison; the results of small scuffles, mostly. The ones that decorated most of her body were often hidden from our view and were formed long before she found me.

Jax's shoulders slumped as she picked through the berry pile. "I know." I felt a twinge in my chest. She wasn't built for this world. She was made to live somewhere beautiful... somewhere safe.

"Did you have to go far to get the berries?" Lucy asked, plucking one from the pile.

"Farther than yesterday," I murmured as she plopped the berry into her mouth.

She nodded. "We'll have to move on soon, find a better area." Before I could say anything she turned and walked off. I watched her go, her long strides carrying her across the camp toward Mason's back. I sighed and sat down beside Jax and began helping her pick debris from the pile.

"Why do we always have to move around?" Her voice was small, fragile. Jax was a porcelain doll; a strong breeze could have shattered her.

"To stay safe." I repeated the words a thousand times before, an explanation to a million other questions she had fired at me, each one a sharpened blade aimed at my heart. I watched her crumple, folding in on herself as the words settled around us. There was no other answer I could give her.

After a few moments of silence, she drew a deep breath and smiled at me. "Do you want to help me pick flowers? I want to make a memorial for the bunny."

I glanced over at Lucy, finding her helping Mason skin the rabbit. When I looked back at Jax, I found her doe eyes staring hopefully at me. "Alright, but we have to be fast. You know how Lucy feels about pointless things."

She nodded excitedly and scrambled to her feet, grinning at me as she headed off toward the trees. "Hurry up, Soph!"

As I dragged myself off the ground to follow her. I waved at Lucy. She simply nodded as she watched Jax disappear into the trees. "Jax slow down," I called. She darted quickly between the trees, stopping only long enough to scoop up the occasional flower as she went. "Jax you can't go so fast, I'm going to lose you." Panic began to bubble inside me as she moved. She was going too fast. Branches snagged my shirt and scratched at my skin as I tried to keep up with her, desperate to keep her in my sight. "Jax wait!" The toe of my boot snagged on a root and sent me ass-over-tea-kettle into the dirt and rotting leaves.

The smell of decay filled my nostrils and choked me as I scrambled to get up. Silence settled over the forest and I turned slowly, listening for the sound of Jax's footsteps. "Jax!" Fear crept into my voice, her name shaking as it left my tongue. "Jax, this isn't funny!" My chest tightened as I spun around again. The once sharp lines of the trees and leaves went fuzzy as a lump formed in my throat. My heart thundered until it was all that I could hear.

"Got you!"

I couldn't help the scream that burst from me as Jax slammed into my back. I twisted around to glare at her. Her giggles washed over me, and my panic was replaced with anger. "What the fuck, Jax?! Are you stupid?" I regretted the words the second I said them, and even more so as I watched the color leave her face, her forehead puckering and the corners of her lips pulling down into a grimace. "Jax— Jax I didn't mean it. I'm sorry. I was just so worried. You can't run off like that. I thought I lost you."

"I'm sorry, Sophia. I just wanted you to smile." She looked so broken, beaten by a world she never should have been forced to live in.

I sighed and pulled her into a hug, burying my face in her sweat-drenched hair. "I know you didn't mean to scare me. I didn't mean to yell at you. I'm sorry."

"It's okay." She stood in my arms just long enough for my heart to stop pounding before she pulled away and offered me the small bouquet of yellow and pink flowers she had collected.

The blossoms smelled sweet and I smiled at her. "Those are beautiful. I'm sure the bunny would've liked them."

"I hope so," she whispered, turning and leading the way back to camp. I followed along behind her, cringing at the way her pace had slowed and the bounce had gone from her gait. A huge part of me crumbled at the memory of Jax's hurt, the way her face had darkened when I yelled at her. It was hard to remember that she was just a child, that the world she had lived in before this was a very sheltered one. The few things she had told us about her life before the end painted the picture of a girl kept in a glass box, something pretty to admire. The end had been Jax's beginning; her first time being out in the world without the iron grip of her parents keeping her from getting hurt. *If only you could put her back in her box.*

When we reentered camp Lucy walked over and smiled softly at Jax. "Are those for the bunny?" Jax beamed at her and nodded, more of her chestnut curls falling from her bun. "I think he would have loved them. Come over here, I had Mason make a memorial for him."

Jax bounded over toward Mason and I leaned closer to Lucy, crossing my arms. "She isn't suited for this world."

Her body tightened and then relaxed with her heavy sigh. "Maybe you're right."

After a brief pause, she slowly made her way toward Jax, a smile pulling one side of her lips up. Jax beamed at her and offered her a small cluster of flowers from her bouquet. Lucy took them and laid them carefully on the makeshift grave before backing away and allowing Jax to lay the rest down. Sometimes I wondered if Lucy was trying to help Jax adjust to the world, or if she was trying to force the world to adjust to Jax.

3

The smell of cooked meat made my mouth water, but I could see Jax's face as she stared into the fire, her nose wrinkling with disgust as the smell wafted around us. With a sigh, I dumped the last of my berries in front of her. I could feel her gaze on me, but I just stared at the flames, the branches collapsing into ashes as they burned.

Albany had fallen like that, crumbling and collapsing in on itself in the wake of the disaster. All of those people meant the shredders were drawn there, the smell of blood luring them like flies to rotting flesh. We tried to stay there, stay close to home, but the waves of monsters pushed us into the wilderness, driving us into the unknown with nothing but the hope that safety lurked in the trees. We passed other camps in our desperate escape attempt; some of them filled with untrusting eyes, others littered with bones and shredded clothes. Looking back, Lucy and I had been foolish to ever believe that we could be safe, but hope was all that we had… our only lifeline as we struggled not to drown.

When everything started getting worse, the suicide rate skyrocketed. Those had been the smart people; they got themselves out, and spared themselves the pain and suffering of this life. *You should have been one of those people.*

"We should move soon."

I jumped before glancing beside me at Lucy and nodding solemnly. The more we moved, the harder we were to hunt. In the firelight, Lucy looked much younger than her 25 years, the golden glow casting shadows that hid the premature wrinkles. When she first found me, she had smooth skin and thick black hair that waved and twisted down her back. I loved her hair, but she insisted that it was trouble and chopped it short with a dull pair of scissors she found in an abandoned house. Now, every few months, she would pull the scissors from her bag and hack at the lengthening strands, cropping them as close to the scalp as she could. *It's almost time for another cut.*

"We just moved," Jax whined, pulling her blanket up under her chin.

"If we don't keep moving we'll end up dead," Lucy huffed at her. She adored Jax but her patience for her was not endless. I couldn't blame her. Jax had boundless energy and the impulse control of a toddler.

"We need to put the fire out." Mason mumbled. He moved to smother the small flame as the sun sank further below the horizon. I always thought that he looked like a bear. He was large and intimidating until you realized that he was afraid of his own shadow. He had gotten better in the last few years, but he was forever cautious.

"Do we have to?" I asked, reaching my hand out toward him and touching his arm to encourage him to leave the flames alone as they started to dwindle.

He sighed, "You know that we do. People will be able to see the light."

"But we haven't seen any other people in weeks," I argued, scooting closer to the barely burning embers, desperate for the comfort of their light.

"Just because we haven't seen them, doesn't mean they aren't out there." If any of us had actually been built for this world, it was Mason.

"When will we be able to stop moving?" Jax's voice was soft, the words almost a whisper.

"I wish I knew," I said absently, looking up at the sky. The stars hung in the air, their arms reaching out toward one another like soul mates reaching for each other's embrace.

"I'll take the first watch," Lucy said, getting to her feet. I nodded and moved to my sleeping bag, snuggling down into it. *The lack of sleep will get you all killed.* It was an unwritten rule that Mason and Jax were not to do patrols. They weren't capable of doing what needed to be done. This far into the mountains, the shredders weren't the main threat, other people were.

Fear was a constant companion and when I finally fell into the darkness, it wrapped me in its familiar embrace as I curled deeper into the folds of my sleeping bag.

"Come out, come out wherever you are!"

My father slammed the door to the bedroom shut and pressed his back to it. "Hide." The room was almost empty, there was nowhere to hide that would save us. Tears burned my skin as they slipped down my cheeks and I stifled a sob. My mother swore as she held the towel tightly to her bleeding arm, the gray fabric stained with crimson. A few drops fell from the corner, landing on the hardwood with a soft plop sound. Everything seemed to fall into hyper-focus as I scanned the room, searching desperately for somewhere, anywhere to hide.

Heavy footsteps made their way down the hallway, a manic laugh bouncing almost playfully through the near-empty house. "Come out, come out wherever you are!" The hair on the back of my neck stood up as the door knob began to turn back and forth. My mom let out a little squeal and the towel fell from her hands, landing with a sickening splat.

Some dark part of me bubbled with anger. It was her fault they were here, her fault that we were all going to die. I tried to swallow it down, choking on the bitter taste of rage.

"It's going to be alright Sophia." My mom's voice rang through the room and I looked at her in disbelief. *Liar.*

The door began to push open, my father being pushed inch by inch as they forced their way in. Hands stained brown with layers of dry blood reached through the growing crack, fingers stretching and searching. Dirty nails found my father's skin and raked themselves down the length of his arm. He groaned as blood beaded on the surface of his skin. They signed his death warrant.

Sweat poured down my face and I jolted upright, my chest heaving. I drew ragged breath after ragged breath. I let my head fall back and stared motionless up at the sky. Stars twinkled like beacons in the dark, glittering across their slowly lightening canvas. The sun would rise soon; the sky was already turning a deep shade of blue. After what felt like an eternity, I glanced around and sighed. *Lucy never came to wake you for your watch.* I always hated when she did that. It made me feel horrible like she didn't trust that I could do it. I asked her about it once but she had just given me a half-hearted, mumbled response. I had my own theories but I doubted that she would ever tell me the truth. Jax and Mason were still asleep when I began rolling my sleeping bag up and shoving it into my backpack.

4

"I'm going to try to find some more berry bushes before we leave," I said as I crept around Jax. She turned in her sleep, clutching the tattered blue whale to her chest as she moved. I barely heard Lucy's grunt of acknowledgment as I scuttled off into the early morning. The air was still and the smell of wet earth filled my nose. Dewdrops smeared across my sleeves as I moved, pushing branches aside as I went.

I froze, a deer in the headlights of a speeding semi-truck. It was a few moments before the hairs on the back of my neck stood up. For the first time that morning, my sleep-deprived brain fully registered that the air was too still, the morning too quiet. No birds were chirping, no small animals scampering through the layers of dead pine needles that littered the ground. Something was very, *very* wrong. *How could you be so stupid?*

Without a second thought, I spun on my heel and began to creep back towards camp, careful to stay quiet as I moved. I exhaled heavily when I heard Jax's voice bounding happily through the cool morning.

"We have to go," I urged quietly, slinking back into the clearing. Everyone looked at me. Mason cocked his head to the side, pausing as he was shoving his favorite blanket back into his bag. Lucy and Jax stared at me from Jax's sleeping space, her hair half pulled up into a tight bun. "We have to go now," I begged.

Lucy set Jax's hairbrush down as a look of horror crossed her face. "The birds," she whispered.

They began shoving their stuff in their bags and hurrying to get to their feet. Jax was the first to be ready, her hair loose and messed from Lucy's half-finished brush job, eyes wide with fear. Mason came lumbering over, slinging his backpack over his shoulders and adjusting the straps. The silence wrapped itself around us like barbed wire, as we hurried through the trees. Branches broke under our feet and I cringed with each snap. The leaves flew past my face as we ran, our outstretched arms trying to force a path to salvation.

Eventually, the sound of birds singing echoed in my ears and the tightness in my chest lessened.

"Wanna play a game?" Jax asked, bounding up beside Mason.

Mason beamed at her. "Sure kiddo. What do you want to play?"

"Eye spy!" Jax yelled, bouncing excitedly from one foot to the other.

Mason shook his head and smiled. "You always want to play that game."

"That's because it's my favorite."

"Alright," Mason chuckled. "Do you want to go first?"

Jax nodded and started scanning the forest. "I spy something," she paused, "yellow!"

Mason squinted as he looked around and I smiled to myself. "Is it that tree?" He pointed towards a large green pine tree.

Jax erupted into a fit of giggling. "That's not yellow! That's green!"

"Is it?" Mason asked with a wry smile. *The perfect big brother.*

"Try again," she urged.

"Hmm," he mused, tapping his chin. "Is it that... flower?" *It's always a flower.*

"Yes! Your turn!"

"Shhh," Lucy hissed, waving her hand. The smile fell from Jax's face and she stepped closer to Mason, hiding in his side. He looked at Lucy, cocking his head. "Listen," she whispered.

More sounds joined the chorus of birds and I strained to hear. *People.* I couldn't make out what they were saying, or how many of them there were. Everything was too muffled and jumbled together.

We stopped as the voices grew louder. Lucy looked at Mason, a silent conversation passing between them. Jax and Mason were too trusting. One fake smile, one almost friendly laugh, and they would be willing to lay down their lives and die for people that would have happily tossed them to the

4

wolves. As though he could read her mind, Mason grabbed Jax's hand and tugged her with him as he moved into a cluster of thicker trees, vanishing into the shadows. I knew he would get her far enough away, somewhere safe to wait for us.

Lucy and I crept closer, a large empty building coming into view. Playground equipment sat rusted and unused, the ghosts of the children that had once used it the only thing that remained. The windows were mostly gone, smashed with jagged bits of glass sticking out. It was collapsing in on itself, the bricks falling onto the cracked sidewalk as the whole place folded in. I didn't see any people around as I strained to listen, their voices growing fainter. Hopefully, they were moving on.

"This could be somewhere to stay for a while," Lucy said, a hint of excitement laced through her words. The thought of somewhere safe made my heart jump, delight flooding me at the very mention of it. "You wait here and keep watch. I'll look inside and see if it's safe."

I nodded and she slunk towards a half-crumbled doorway, vanishing into the darkness of the building. *Jax will be so excited.* I knew it wasn't smart to think about the joy that Jax would feel at being able to call somewhere home, but I couldn't help it. I would give anything to make sure they were safe.

I sat behind the bushes for a few moments, prematurely making plans for a building that might not even be an option. I stiffened as the sound of voices drifted to me, and I peered through the leaves, straining to see if the people had returned. Silhouettes stalked into the darkness where Lucy had vanished and dread settled in the pit of my stomach. *What if they find her?* I knew that Mason and I couldn't take care of Jax on our own. We needed Lucy. She was our protector, the only one of us that never seemed to lose sight of what was important and what was at stake.

Once the voices faded until I could no longer hear them, I crept over to the nearest row of shattered windows and carefully climbed inside, hoping that I would find Lucy before they did.

The building stunk of mold and death, the sour smell burning my nose to the point that my eyes started to water. Broken glass, dried blood, and dirt covered the tile floors; a reminder of the horrible things that this building bore witness to. The walls were littered with scratches, some of them tinged with ancient brown blood stains. The doors lining the hallway were all open, sunlight from beyond them streaming out across the narrow space. I glanced into a few of the rooms. Only horror greeted me. Empty desks were thrown about, papers rotting from the elements. Blood covered the walls like paint, the sickly stains flaking off the dirty white bricks and falling like snow onto the floor.

I crept through the hallways, desperate to find Lucy. I was hyper-aware of the thump of my boots on the dirt-covered floors. After I scanned a few of the rooms, I spotted her footprints in the layer of dirt that coated the tile. *Lucy.* Relief surged through me as I followed them into a classroom. They stopped at a counter suspiciously lacking dust and glass despite the broken window above it. She must have heard the others come in and got out before they found her. I stretched to peer out and saw a lattice laying in pieces at the base of the hill. This side of the building was too high for me to jump from the window without the lattice to climb down. *Shit.* It must have broken when Lucy was trying to get out.

I turned and scrambled back out into the hallway, retracing my steps. All I had to do was get back outside. I rounded a corner and froze. They stared at me for a second, as if they, too, were shocked to see another person. But then sickening smiles spread across their faces.

I ran.

Desperate to escape, I took turn after turn until I couldn't breathe. The hallways seemed endless, each twist leading to another. A small alcove offered at least a little protection. I crouched down and tried to catch my breath.

The cool brick stole the warmth from my skin as I pressed myself against it, flattening as much as I could. I should have listened to Lucy. I should have stayed where I was and just waited... or I should have just sucked it up and jumped out that window. *Stupid girl.* I covered my mouth with one hand, trying to muffle my breathing, terrified that they would hear me. I could hear their footsteps, the heavy pounding of their boots echoing through the destroyed halls as they hunted me.

"Come out, come out wherever you are!" his voice called. My breath

4

hitched in my throat at the sound of those words, ice creeping through my veins as I tried to swallow fear. The sound was raspy and menacing, calling forth memories of the villains in my favorite childhood movies. Chills raced up my spine and I could feel the tears on my cheeks. The pit in my stomach grew, and I laid my head back against the wall, cursing myself again for being stupid. A laugh echoed through the dim hall and I pressed myself harder against the wall. Their footsteps grew closer, leaves and broken glass crunching under their weight.

"We just want to talk to you!" a different voice sang out. I wasn't sure how many of them there were and I wasn't eager to find out. In the darkness, I could make out some of the debris that littered the floor and I swore inwardly, pulling my feet closer to my body. I stared at the wall across from me and wrapped my arms around my knees. *They'll see you.* The walls on either side of me felt like they were shrinking, and I fumbled to make myself smaller. In my desperation, my boot smacked something and sent it skidding across the floor.

My breath hitched in my throat and I struggled not to choke on it as panic tore into me. *You fucked up.*

They were going to find me. There was no way they wouldn't see me. When I heard their voices again, they were muffled, soft... they were whispering to one another. *They saw you otherwise, they would have moved on by now.* I drew a shaky breath and decided I'd rather die fighting than sitting and waiting for it. I pushed myself up the length of the wall slowly and prepared to run. If I was fast enough, I could make it back outside before them and I would be able to slip back into the trees. They wouldn't find me among the fallen logs and towering pines.

I counted to three in my head, sliding further out of my hiding spot with each number. When I hit three, I started running, blindly racing down the long hallway toward what I hoped was freedom. I heard them start to chase me, their heavy footfalls right behind me. I rounded a corner into a large open room and sunlight washed over me from the large picture window on the far wall. I was going to make it. I was only feet from freedom when the air burst from my lungs in a desperate scream as I was yanked backward.

The world spun as I went sprawling and skidding across the floor. Rocks and broken bits of glass cut at my skin leaving small smears of blood in the dirt. I hurriedly tried to get to my feet to search for a different route to escape, but it was too late. They had me like an animal in a trap. They looked at me with hungry expressions, their lips curling up into predatory sneers.

5

"Well look at what we have here Luke. A little mouse."

They laughed and inched closer to me. *Wolves closing in on a lamb.* I scanned the room quickly and noticed a small doorway on the opposite wall from the window. Freedom. Their large frames moved into my line of sight, one slightly in front of the other, blocking the doorway. I glared at them and tried to run. I slipped past one only for a searing pain to rip through my scalp, his warm fingers knotting in the short blonde strands. He threw me back onto the floor between them.

"A feisty little mouse," the other chuckled.

"Don't worry, we can take the fight out of her."

I slid away from them until my back was against the wall. I wouldn't let them sneak up on me. *Don't look away from them.* Blindly, I searched the floor for something, anything to defend myself. My fingers touched the jagged edge of something cold and I clutched it in my hand, squeezing until it cut into my palm. Glass. Slowly, I tucked my feet under myself and moved into a crouched position. They were closing in on me, stalking closer with each one of my panicked heartbeats. This time when I ran, I swung at the first one that reached for me. His blood was warm as it rushed down the glass and onto my hand and arm. He laughed; the low, amused sound make the hairs on the back of my neck stand up. *Who laughs when they're hurt?*

"You bitch!" When he grabbed me, he didn't let go. He must have been at least a head taller than me. One arm snaked around my waist and held me against his body while the other pried at my fingers, bending them until I dropped the glass. It shattered when it hit the floor, spraying across the dirty ground and shining in the few flashes of sunlight that streamed through the large broken window. *Fight.* I clawed at his arms, my nails digging into his skin until I smelled the coppery scent of blood. He dropped me and before I could run again his boot slammed into my stomach, making me curl in on myself and knocking the air from my lungs. It felt like I was suffocating as I tried to breathe to no avail. I was going to die here, or at the very least, I was going to wish that I had. I felt the fear coil in the pit of my stomach and I looked up at their faces as they loomed over me. They were human, but there was no humanity left in them.

"Don't worry, little mouse. We won't hold that stunt against you." *Liar.*

"Get away from me!" They both laughed as I tried to sit up. One of their boots caught me in the side and knocked me back down. My head snapped back as the other tangled his hands in my hair.

His breath was hot and wet against my ear. "I don't appreciate the cut, little girl." Shivers ran up my spine and I bit down on my tongue to avoid crying. *Don't give them the satisfaction.* Something flashed in the corner of my eye and then a sharp pain shot through my body as my blood rushed hot and sticky down my face and neck. "Now we can match," he hissed. I felt his tongue against my cheek, following along the gash. My stomach turned, bile rising in my throat. The pain radiated from my chin, up past my lip, and stopped somewhere on my cheek, though exactly where I couldn't tell. In the dying light, the ground shone with patches of brilliant scarlet. A different kind of panic set in. *There's too much blood.* They would smell it.

"I have to go," I rasped. A stunned silence fell over the room and I tried to wiggle free, pulling what felt like chunks of my hair out in my desperation. *They'll grow back.*

"Oh no you don't." The wind was knocked from me again as he slammed me onto the floor. My stomach and chest screamed in pain, the tiny shards of broken glass embedding themselves into my skin. *More blood.*

"You don't understand," I gasped breathlessly. "They'll smell the blood. They'll come here looking for food."

"Do you think she's right?" the one that had been holding me asked. I could hear the fear beginning to creep into him, sinking its claws in.

"She's just trying to get away. We haven't seen any sign of those damn things in weeks."

"I saw one this morning. Not far from here," I begged, getting up onto my knees and trying to stand. I prayed that they believed the lie. I hadn't *seen* one, but I knew they were there. I knew they were getting close. Even the animals knew that those things were dangerous; nature held its breath when they were near.

"Maybe we should listen to her," one offered.

The other sighed and wrapped a strong hand around my arm, yanking me to my feet, and dragging me closer to him. "You win," he growled into my ear, "but you stay with us. And if we run into one of those things, you're the sacrifice. Understand?" I nodded and he grumbled an acknowledgment before barking at his partner, "Hand me your lighter."

I knew what was coming now. They had to stop the bleeding.

I struggled to see their faces in the dim light, their features mostly cloaked in shadow. He kicked at the floor, searching. The telltale sound of boot against metal echoed through the quiet room. He stooped down and a spoon flashed silver in the light from a sunbeam. He held it to the flame until it became red with heat. His free hand wrapped around my head, his large palm smacking into the back of my skull and holding me captive. I jerked away as searing pain bit into my face and a quick hiss filled my ears. My eyes watered and I squealed, thrashing in his grip. A sickening smell like charcoal and sulfur wrapped around me and swam in my brain, my vision going blurry.

I sat clumsily on the floor while he cauterized his friend's face. I could hear the hiss of the metal touching his skin and I braced for sounds of pain.

There was silence.

It settled around us, turning the humid summer air to ice. *Something is very wrong with one of them.*

My vision was still hazy as they pulled me back onto my feet and nudged me toward the large window that had moments ago been my escape route. I stumbled towards what had once been hope but was now surely a death sentence. The sunlight was blinding and my head throbbed as I struggled to adjust.

I was shoved forward and almost fell face-first into the grass. "Move!" he barked at me. I looked back at them and for the first time really studied their faces. They had to be brothers. Their faces were too similar to be anything but. The one I cut was the smaller of the two, his tanned skin littered with large, jagged scars. The larger one was the aggressor, his face freckled from his time in the sun, his brown eyes hard and unfeeling. "Hurry up!" he snapped. Before I turned back around something scribbled on the side of the crumbling building caught my attention:

Eden Welcomes All Survivors.

The words under the main message were much smaller but my captors shoved me forward before I could finish reading. I stumbled on unsteady feet toward the forest. *Eden?* As we drew nearer to the trees, I scanned them for Lucy. *Had she seen the message?* I thought I spotted her, but before I could look back to double-check, the leaves swallowed us. *Would she take Jax and Mason there?*

6

The sun was at the highest point in the sky by the time we stopped walking. The muscles in my legs quivered from the hike across the uneven terrain, sweat rolling down my face and the back of my neck. I collapsed into a heap on the soft bed of pine needles, tucking myself into the shade from a large tree. I watched my captors silently. They appeared to be ignoring me. *Don't run. If you try, they'll catch you.*

"Alright, little mouse," the younger one began. He turned to face me, and I was met with piercing blue eyes. "We're safe."

The older one snorted, "You and I are safe. Unfortunately, I can't say the same for her." He looked at me. "You still haven't paid for cutting my baby brother." *You were right.*

"He cut me back," I growled. "I think that's payment enough."

They both laughed before the older one spoke. "You wish." He stalked closer to me, his movements fluid and smooth. *How many girls came before you?* I scurried away from him, flipping onto my stomach and crawling through the needles. Hidden rocks and broken branches stabbed into my palms and knees. I tried to get my feet under me, but his hand grabbed the back of my shirt and I heard the fabric tear. I wobbled, thrown off balance, and froze as I hit my knees to steady myself. The warm sunlight washed over a small patch of my bare skin and he made a *tsk* sound, his tongue clicking as he traced the wounds the glass left behind. I lurched forward, one last attempt at freedom. He smacked my back with a sickening thump, driving me back into the dirt.

"Let me go!" I screamed, thrashing.

He pressed me painfully into the ground, the smell of sweat making me nauseous as it dripped onto me. I turned my head to avoid suffocating and he put his face close to mine, his lips almost touching my skin. "Never, little mouse," he whispered. I blinked the tears away. *Don't let them see you cry.* "It's been a long time since we found a toy as pretty as you."

A sickening feeling washed over me and settled in the pit of my stomach. I struggled to get away, wiggling to free myself from his crushing weight. My blood ran cold when I heard the deep throaty groan. *You've made a terrible mistake.* I bit my tongue and swallowed the scream as his calloused hands found the top of my jeans and slipped under me, moving toward the button and zipper.

"Please don't," I whispered. My plea was met with a rumbling laugh and another set of hands exploring my skin. These hands were gentle as they brushed the hair from my face. I looked up. Pale eyes stared down into mine, the jagged gash across his face weeping blood again. *I hope he dies from infection.*

The younger one touched the cut on my face softly, wiping the blood from around it. He almost looked sad. *Help me,* I mouthed the words at him, begging… hoping that his gentle touch meant there was some humanity left in him. He shook his head and then smiled—a smile that didn't reach his eyes. He moved his index finger to my lips and slowly spread my blood across my bottom one. He flashed a dimpled grin before sticking the finger into his mouth, the hollows of his cheeks sinking in as he sucked my blood off. A groan fell from his lips and his eyes slid closed. My stomach turned and I tried to look away from him, vomit rising up the back of my throat. I swallowed it down when he grabbed my chin and squeezed until I yelped. The button of my jeans popped open and my whole body went cold.

"You will look at me. Do you understand?" I struggled in his grip, trying to yank my head free. "Do." His face drew closer to mine. "You." He squeezed harder as I struggled to turn away from him. "Understand." *He's too close.* His lips were almost touching mine when he whispered, "I am your only chance for survival." He laughed, a deep menacing sound. "My brother will kill you."

The weight pressing down on me lessened. He ripped the fabric over my

6

hips and down my legs. Now all that stood between me and him were a thin pair of cotton underwear. His weight returned, pressing me further down into the dirt. The warmth of his bare skin touching mine sent chills through me. His breath crawled across my skin and his tongue grazed my ear, making me gag. *You are going to suffer.*

"Why don't you just get it over with?" I spat.

The younger one chuckled and pressed one finger to the tip of my nose, grinning.

"Where's the fun in that?" the older one whispered against my ear, biting the lobe. This will be slow. "But I might let you live if you do exactly what you're told." *Will you want to after this?*

"Just let me go," I begged, looking at the one in front of me.

Blue eyes glittered with amusement as he moved his finger from my nose to my lips, tracing their shape slowly.

"It's not that bad, little mouse." He kissed my neck, biting hard enough to make me wince. "You could be torn apart by one of those monsters." He lifted a strand of my hair and rolled it around in his fingers. "I heard when they're done, there isn't anything left except pieces of skin and bone."

"I'd rather take my chances with them," I hissed through clenched teeth.

He pulled my hair, yanking my head back and away from his brother. He rose off me just enough to stare down into my face. "I'll hurt you even worse if you don't behave." Tears stung my eyes and I pulled away from him, ripping my hair from his grasp. I pushed up from the dirt with my hands and tried to roll to throw him off. *Fight.* He grabbed my throat. *Fight.* I opened my mouth to scream but all that came out was a wheeze, his fingers tightening until there was no air. The strength slowly left my body and I fell limp in his grasp. "Stop fighting so hard," he grumbled.

The younger one tugged at his fingers and he loosened his grip. "Don't kill her Christopher. I want to keep her." He laid down on his stomach in the dirt and stared into my face, smiling.

"I'm not a pet," I wheezed.

My face was shoved into the dirt and I yelped in shock.

"You'll be whatever I decide," Christopher said bluntly. "I'll think about it,

Luke. But she's probably more trouble than she's worth." He grabbed the thin cotton that separated us and tore it from my body. I stifled my scream as he allowed me to turn my head and draw a shaky breath. "That doesn't mean we can't take our time and have fun with her though."

I couldn't stop the few tears that managed to slip loose. Luke wiped them away with his thumb. Christopher groaned as pain ripped through my abdomen and my thighs grew slick with what I could only assume was blood. This had to be some kind of divine punishment; the sentence I'd earned being paid out early. *Maybe you'll make it into Heaven after all.*

He put his face close to mine. "You feel great." His voice was throaty and I laid frozen, yearning for death.

I stared motionless into Luke's face as it hovered close to mine, wishing the shadows in his gaze would swallow me and put me out of my misery. *You should have waited for Lucy.* Luke inched closer to me. *Now you're going to die.*

His tongue flicked out and licked the length of his bottom lip. "The things I have in store for you," he moaned. He reached out to touch my face, slowly walking two of his fingers from chin to temple. *Monster.*

After a small eternity, Christopher's body weight left me. I was too frightened to move.

"She isn't trying to run, Christopher. Can we keep her?" Luke lifted a strand of my hair and twirled it around his finger. "I've always wanted a blonde."

"I suppose if she keeps behaving herself we can." Christopher walked past me, fidgeting with his belt.

"I'm not a pet," I snapped softly, my fight beginning to fade.

Christopher kicked dirt at me and I closed my eyes. "You're whatever the fuck I say you are." The venom dripped from his words. "Hurry up Luke, we don't have all day."

"You didn't have to hurry," Luke protested, brushing the dirt from my face and hair.

"Just do what I say," Christopher sighed. "We have to get back."

Luke huffed and got to his feet, undoing his jeans before he walked behind me. Weight once again pressed me down into the dirt and I felt another piece

6

of my soul die. "I'm sorry," Luke whispered, brushing the hair away from the right side of my face. "I promise not to hurt you." His lips touched my cheek softly and I fought the urge to jerk my face away. *Don't make them mad.* Everything went cold. *You should have been one of the floods of suicides.* Luke's fingers lightly traced my face, running along my bottom lip and trying to force me to open my mouth. *You should have ended everything long ago.* He trailed kisses across my shoulders, biting at my skin as he went. *Stupid girl.* He grabbed a fist full of my hair and ripped my head back, biting down on the tender spot between the base of my neck and my shoulder hard enough to draw blood. *Dead girl.*

His front teeth sank into the hollow spot above my collarbone while his bottom teeth cut deep into my back. I arched up, blood forming small rivers over my shoulder and dripping into the dirt. I fought the scream that slammed into the back of my teeth as pain ripped me apart from the inside out.

He finally crawled off of me. The sun was beginning to sink below the trees, shadows extending themselves across the forest floor and touching me with their comforting embrace.

"Get up and put these on." A heap of clothes landed beside my head and I groggily dragged myself into a sitting position. I glanced at Christopher as he zipped the faded blue backpack closed and swung it onto his shoulder. My shaky hands reached out and grabbed the clothing, slipping the sweatpants and oversized shirt on. *Maybe they'll leave you here.* "We should get moving. Our camp isn't far from here." My boots plopped onto the ground beside me and I slid them on before Christopher gruffly pulled me onto my feet and shoved me forward. "Walk."

"Be gentle with her," Luke cooed, grabbing my elbow to steady me.

"You weren't," Christopher grumbled.

I stumbled hazily along through the trees, my legs still sticky with blood. *Maybe you'll attract the shredders.* My shoulder throbbed where Luke bit me, the blood still running down my back. *Maybe they'll tear Luke and Christopher apart.* Not long after the sun disappeared below the horizon, a semi-circle of tents came into view and the soft murmur of voices washed over me. A group of three was sitting lazily around a small fire, their faces lit by the fire as they spotted me and my attackers.

"Luke! Christopher!" a middle-aged man called, waving. "You pick up another stray?"

Christopher grabbed my arm and squeezed until I winced. "You say anything about what happened and I'll make it so much worse next time. Understand?" I nodded and his hand dropped. "Yeah, we found her wandering around the old school. She was all alone and hurt pretty bad. Figured she'd be better off with us."

"Luke, what happened to your face?!" a small brunette gasped, flitting up to Luke. She was like a pixie, moving a thousand miles a minute as she examined the cut, her little fingers touching and probing before she pressed her lips to his cheek and grabbed his hand. "We have to get it cleaned up before you get an infection." I stared at him blankly as he shuffled off toward the tents with her and I was left standing with Christopher.

"What happened to her face?" the man asked, looking at me closely. I held my breath as his face hovered near mine. His forehead wrinkled as he leaned in closer and examined the cut, his breath hot on my skin.

"She freaked out when we first found her and got cut pretty bad in the scuffle, but not before she got Luke." His arm wrapped around my shoulders before he pulled me into his body, tucking me away from the scrutinizing gaze of the man. I stared at him desperately, hoping he'd see through the lies he was being fed and help me, begging him to notice the panic and desperation on my face. *Please.*

"You should have Rachel clean it. It's going to get infected if you don't." His eyes remained fixed on me as he said the words. My mind urged me to ask him for help, to run at him and beg him to save me, but something held me in place. My fear rooted me to the ground and I watched the man turn and leave, my only chance at escape walking off. *Stupid. You deserve to die. You can't even fight for your own life.* I hung my head as Christopher's grip on me loosened.

"Rachel!" I jumped as his frame vibrated when he called for her.

7

Their camp was small; only four tents sitting in a haphazard semi-circle around the fire pit. *Yours is almost the same size.* After a few seconds, a female voice echoed in my ears. "What, Christopher?" Her tone was hard... cold.

"She has a cut. It needs to be cleaned up."

"And?" She sounded irritated.

He sighed, the muscles in his body tensing with anger. She was poking the bear. "Can you clean it?" The words were sharp, each one spat at her.

"Can you ask properly?"

I turned my head to look at the woman and found a small redhead glaring at Christopher. Her caramel eyes burned into him, her forehead wrinkled deeply with her frown.

"Can you *please* clean her cut Rachel?" His voice was tight as he ground out the words like venom on his tongue.

A smug smile spread across her face and she nodded. "Of course I can." She looked at me now and the smile dropped from her lips. The lines in her forehead returned, though they looked deeper than before. She frowned hard at me. "What happened to you?" Her voice softened as she spoke to me. *She feels bad for you.* She was regarding me the same way that I regarded wounded animals.

"She freaked out when we found her and cut her face on some metal. Just clean it." He was agitated with this girl, this Rachel.

Her expression steeled again as she glared up at him. "Did I ask you, Christopher?" She held her hand out to me and I reached for it, desperate for some kind of lifeline. *She could be your salvation.*

Before I could touch her, Christopher's nails bit into my arm and he put his lips to my ear. "If you tell her anything, I'll kill you. I don't care what my baby brother says." Chills ran down my spine as he pressed his lips to my skin and finally loosened his grip. *The picture-perfect savior and the broken wounded thing he saved.*

I grabbed Rachel's hand like a life preserver, clinging onto it to keep myself from sinking as she towed me along behind her. My fingers tightened around hers, holding on to the only chance of survival I had.

Her tent was small, allowing barely enough headroom for us to stand up in the very center. Boxes and bags littered the space along the walls, haphazardly lined up to make as much room for her small sleeping bag as possible. She cleared her throat as she faced me. "What did they do to you?" I was taken aback by the question and pinwheeled in my mind to find a suitable answer. *This is what you have been waiting for.* I opened my mouth to speak, prepared to blurt out the entire story, to rip open my soul and bare the darkest parts of it to this girl, but I choked. The words turned to ashes in my mouth and I gagged on the sour taste.

"N—nothing," I stuttered. *Weak.*

She snorted. "I'm not stupid. Do you think I don't know they're fucking monsters?" She raised her eyebrows. "Now, what did they do to you?" I stared at her, opening and closing my mouth like a fish ripped from the water. Fear gripped me. *What if they find out you told her?* The things that they had done to me tore me apart, but the things that they could still do to me frightened me into silence. Her eyes softened and she touched my hand. "I can't help you if you don't tell me."

"You can't help me anyway," I whispered, bowing my head and sinking to the floor of the tent. *Pathetic.* The chance to save myself was handed to me on a silver platter and I was too weak to take it.

"I can if you let me."

I looked up at her. "How?" My voice sounded alien to me; too meek… too desperate.

"Well," she began, "we can start by making sure that you don't die of an infection. Then we can figure out how we are going to get you out of here."

She rummaged around in a small box beside the door until she emerged with a bottle of reddish liquid, a syringe, a glass vial of something clear, and a cloth. "This might sting a bit." I nodded as she readied the cloth with the dark liquid. She knelt down in front of me and offered a sad smile. "I'm sorry," she whispered, reaching toward me with the cloth. When it touched the cut on my cheek it felt like liquid fire, eating away at the tender skin and I winced. I took a sharp breath through my teeth. "I have to get all the dirt off. What did he use to stop the bleeding?"

"Hot metal," I bit out, grinding my teeth as she continued to scrub at my skin. It felt like acid burning away the layers of the injury and creating one of its very own.

"Hopefully the heat killed the bacteria, but just in case I'm going to give you some antibiotics." I nodded and she moved on to the syringe and the glass vial. "This won't sting as badly, I promise." *Sting? Is that what she called it?* The prick of the needle was nothing compared to the horrors of the day and when she was done she smiled. "What's your name?"

"Sophia."

"Is that your real name?" She arched an eyebrow that didn't quite match the fiery mane of hair.

"Yes."

"Are you going to tell it to them?"

I stared at her blankly. "No."

"Are you going to try to get out of here?"

"Yes." I jerked, startled by my answer. I hadn't thought. Instead, I said the first thing that popped into my head, letting it roll off my tongue before I fully realized what I was admitting. I had trusted her with my name, but trusting her with an admission of trying to leave was dangerous. *What if she tells them?*

"Do you want my help?"

Do you? "Yes." She nodded at my answer and began to dig through a bag before offering me a new set of clothes. I took them and smiled at her. "Thank you."

"Don't mention it. Let me tell you something about Christopher and

Luke." I nodded as I stripped off their clothing and replaced it with Rachel's. "Luke is a follower. He's a little unhinged on his own, but he isn't dangerous without Christopher." *She obviously didn't meet the same Luke you did.* "But Christopher..." her voice trailed off. Something about her face, about the way storm clouds darkened her sunshine eyes, made my heart ache.

"He hurt you didn't he?"

She jumped a little. "No, not me. Someone—someone else." Her voice was distant as the weight of her pain settled in the stagnant air between us. I didn't push her. She had her own demons to fight and I had mine.

My shoulder screamed in agony as I pulled the sweatshirt over my head and dropped it on the ground. *He bit you.* "Rachel?" I asked tentatively. *It's going to get infected.*

"Hmmm?" She was already putting away the vials, hunched over the box on the far side of the tent.

"Can you look at one more thing for me?"

She glanced at me. "Sure, what?" I took a deep breath, got onto my knees, and turned so my back was facing her. "Oh," she breathed, taking a small step back. "What bit you?" *She thinks you're infected.*

There was fear in her voice and I whipped around quickly to face her. "Luke," I blurted.

"Luke did this?" She made a twirling motion with her finger and I turned back around. Her hands were cold when she touched the skin around the bite. It felt nice. "I'll clean it." Her tiny glass vials clinked together and I braced myself for the bite of whatever she had used on my face. "I'm sorry," she murmured, pressing the liquid-soaked cloth to the torn skin. *Fuck.* It felt like my skin was melting off as she dabbed at the bite mark. "I'm not going to stitch it. It isn't that deep." I nodded, swallowing a scream. "The antibiotics I already gave you should help keep it from getting infected. I'll look at it again tomorrow just to make sure. We can give you another shot if needed." My skin was still on fire even after she put the cloth away. "I'll just put something over it to keep it clean." Tears dammed behind my lashes and I blinked rapidly to get rid of them. *Don't cry.* She taped a large piece of gauze to my shoulder and then allowed me to finish getting dressed.

8

When we emerged from the tent, the fire in the center of the camp was much larger than it had been earlier. An ocean of stars filled the sky above our heads and I took a deep breath of the cool night air. I scanned the group of people and found the older man staring at me, the corners of his lips pulled down in a hard frown. I stared back unblinking.

"That's Michael," Rachel whispered beside me. "He's always been suspicious of the brothers, but he's never been able to prove anything."

"Prove what exactly?"

"They're killers," Rachel said bluntly.

I snorted, "Why prove it? Just do what needs to be done."

"That's not how it works here Sophia," Rachel snipped. I nodded, biting my tongue and making my way toward the fire. *They have rules. How odd.* People were usually more than happy to play judge, jury, and executioner. Luke and the pretty brunette from earlier were sitting together not far from Michael, his arms wrapped tightly around her waist, her sitting snuggly in his lap. "That's Mara. Luke and Christopher came back with her almost a year ago and she's been glued to Luke ever since."

Mara reached to brush her hair back from her face and the scars on her arms glistened in the firelight. She offered me a sad smile, her hazel eyes almost empty, as if all the life inside of her had been sucked right out. *They're parasites.*

"What happened to her arms?" I whispered, glancing at Rachel.

"She always said she was clumsy. She'd come to me every other day asking for a bandage or stitches. It would always be a new cut or a bruise. I knew they weren't from falling, but," she took a deep breath, "she would never tell me what they did to her." She bit her bottom lip, tilting her head slightly and staring into the distance.

"Will she be alright, Rachel?"

I flinched at the sound of Christopher's voice, my skin prickling.

"Probably." Rachel bristled.

"Thanks." He seized my arm and squeezed. I could feel the skin bruising and I winced inwardly. I smiled at Rachel who glared at Christopher before moving off and plopping down next to Michael. "You didn't tell her anything did you?" He squeezed harder, jerking me closer.

"Do you think I'm stupid?" *Probably.*

He squeezed my arm harder. "Yeah, actually I do." *Scream. Tell the world what monsters they truly are.* I remained unmoving, glowering at the dark silhouette of the trees around us. "Come on." He tugged at me as he stalked back to where he was sitting, dragging me along behind him like a rag doll. I followed, tripping and fumbling the whole way, drawing everyone's gazes to us. When he flopped onto the ground, he pulled me down next to him gently, gentler than he had yet to touch me. *Pretender.* Once he settled me beside him, he snaked his arm behind my back and pulled me painfully close to him, leaning to whisper in my ear. "Stop it."

"Stop what?" I asked, looking up at him. Tendrils of messy brown hair were falling into his eyes, and he reached toward them. I jerked, my eyes closing tightly as I prepared myself for the hit that never came. *Breathe.* Christopher's arm tightened around me, his nails digging into my side.

"Sophia?" Rachel asked. I peeked over at her. Her large caramel eyes were locked on me, her fingers reaching into the pocket of her jacket. *Stop saying my name.* "Sophia, are you alright?" *Please stop saying my name.* She snapped her mouth shut and her eyes went wide, realization seemingly dawning on her. *I'm sorry* she mouthed to me.

I slowly straightened myself. "I'm alright." Her gaze lingered on me, eyes darting knowingly to his fingers clawing into my skin through the fabric of the shirt. The air was heavy with tension and I shifted uncomfortably in my seat.

8

"So," Michael began, breaking the momentary silence. I glanced at him, cocking my head, and he smiled at me. "How did you end up running into Christopher and Luke?" I could see the worry bubbling just beneath his surface.

Beside me, Christopher clawed into my skin harder and I bit down on my tongue to avoid crying out. *Don't make him mad.* "I got separated from my group and was just trying to find them," I explained.

"You have a group?" Michael asked, his eyes boring into me.

"Yes."

"When did you get separated from them? *How* did you get separated?" His questions were starting to sound more like demands.

"It wasn't long ago. One of those things was coming after us and when we ran we all went in different directions. I went back and tried to find them, but they were gone." I sighed deeply, and stared at Michael, urging him to see the fear in my eyes.

"You mean you actually got away from one of those monsters?" *And walked right into the waiting arms of two others.*

I nodded sheepishly and looked down at my hands. "I just ran. I didn't do anything."

"How close were you to it?" It was Rachel's voice this time. "What do they look like? I've never seen one up close."

I bit the inside of my cheek for a moment before I responded, "I saw two of them before my parents died." The memory sent shivers down my spine. I'd seen them through the front windows of the house, their clothing dripping with blood as it hung from their emaciated frames, their eyes wild with hunger. "They looked... *almost* human, but one that was starving. They were so thin and frail-looking. I remember wondering why we were afraid of something that looked like it would crumble if you touched it. They moved so fast though, their faces always turned up towards the sky."

"Why?" The question came from Mara, still curled tightly in Luke's lap. Her eyes were wide, her fingers knotted in Luke's shirt. My gaze drifted to his face. Cold blue eyes were locked on me, the hint of a smile playing at his lips.

"Smelling, I'm assuming," I said, glancing back at Mara. "They were covered in blood, it was dripping off of them and leaving a trail. Their skin... it was so pale and flaking in places, like it was chapped. Their eyes were wide and panicked, rimmed with red and purple." My mind began to drag me down into its depths. I could see them clearly in front of me.

"Did they just walk past?" Rachel's voice held a hint of concern like she could sense the dread growing in the pit of my stomach.

"No." I held my breath as they passed my house. My mother was in the kitchen... I heard her swear. She never swore. I turned around just long enough to check on her. She was covered in blood... it was pouring down her arm and dripping onto the floor... She dropped the knife and the sound of it hitting the linoleum was so loud that I knew they heard it. My father rushed to her with a towel. I whipped back to the window. A set of red-rimmed eyes stared straight at me.

Her lips pulled back from her teeth in a wide grin, her hair matted thickly with blood. Her cheeks were hollow, the skin collapsing in on itself, bones jutting out everywhere. She lifted her finger and tapped on the glass, laughing like she was playing with a fish in a bowl. They smelled her. She was so close, I could have touched her.

"They can talk, you know. She called out to us when she got in. I can still hear her voice. It sounded wrong... empty. She laughed while she chased us like it was some kind of game... like she was enjoying it." *Come out, come out wherever you are.* She sang the words, stalking us through the house. I knew she was following the scent of my mother's blood. I heard their feet on the wood and the soft plop of each drop of blood as it hit the floor. Hiding wouldn't save mom, nothing would now that they knew where she was. Heavy knocks sounded on the door. That laugh grew high in pitch. Manic. The door knob turned faster then stopped.

"So what happened to your face?" The voice jolted through me. I blinked through the firelight as my heartbeat slowed. Michael's intent stare slowly came into focus. Everything blurred together but slowly came into focus. His forehead scrunched up, making the wrinkles even deeper than before. My face was hot, sweat beading on my brow despite the cool night air.

8

"I tripped and fell when I was running through the school." I was lost in a haze, my head swimming from the ebbing adrenaline the memory flooded me with. "But Luke's cut," I began, "I'm the one that gave him that." Michael's eyes widened as he stared at me and I saw Luke shift uncomfortably from the corner of my eye. A sick sense of satisfaction settled itself into my brain, pumping me full of false confidence. *Stupid girl.* I made the big bad wolf uncomfortable.

"Yeah," Christopher chuckled awkwardly, "she got him good. We did scare her at first though. Two strange men and all." He rubbed his face with his free hand. *Trying to wipe away the guilt.*

I flashed a small smile at all of them. "Sorry, Luke."

I settled my gaze on him and he stared right back, a smile tugging at the corner of his lips. "It's alright, *Sophia.*" My name floated off of his tongue like a serpent, venom dripping from its fangs. *You fucked up.* His eyes drifted down the length of my body, and I squirmed under his gaze. Out of the corner of my eye, Rachel shifted in her seat, sinking down into it and refusing to look at me.

"Well," Christopher began, "I'm sure she's awfully tired after today so I'll just get her settled so she can sleep." He stood up, pulling me along with him and dragging me towards the tents. His was the farthest from the fire and I swallowed hard as we drew closer to it. He nudged me inside and followed behind me, zipping the door shut and closing out the others.

I wasn't ready when his hand made contact with my face and I crumpled to the floor. The world spun and my stomach lurched as I scrambled away from him. He reached out and dragged me back to him, wrapping his hand around my throat and pulling my face close to his. "I will kill you."

9

His threat sat in the stagnant air between us. *Don't poke the bear.* "Then do it," I rasped, struggling for air as his hand tightened. *Idiot.*

His expression darkened. "I'll do you one worse." He wrestled me down, pressing me with his weight until I was flat on my back, his large frame looming over me. *No.* I thrashed in his grip but he squeezed until the edges of my vision began to grow blurry. I stilled beneath him and he released a bit of the pressure. His free hand tugged at the fabric of Rachel's leggings until they tore. He clawed at the remnants, pulling them away from my skin until I was left exposed to his hungry eyes once again. *Please no.* He walked his fingers slowly up my bare legs, leaving goosebumps in their wake. He smiled cruelly down at me. "Killing you would make you too happy."

I stared too long into the darkness of his gaze. Hatred and anger swelled in the depths, an uncontrolled ocean that threatened to swallow everything in its path. *He will consume you.* He trailed a finger down the good side of my face, tracing the skin between my eye and the corner of my lips.

His hold on my throat loosened a little more and I took a deep breath. "Please let me go," I whispered. He shook his head slowly and returned the pressure to my neck, *tsking.*

"You need to learn to be quiet, little mouse." He reached down to his waistband, popping the button on his jeans and wiggling them down over his hips. I squeezed my eyes shut and wiggled in his grasp as he pressed his weight down on me again, trying to get away. My lungs burned and my head swam from the lack of oxygen. Maybe he'd kill me by accident. *That's all you can hope for at this point.* His skin was hot when it touched mine and my stomach turned, bile rising in my chest. Fear gripped me in its claws, digging deep into my soul and ripping out the pulpy bits. I squeezed my legs shut but he forced them open and shoved himself between them. I felt his breath on my face and neck as he leaned in close. "I wish I could hear you scream when I do this."

He pushed inside of me and another piece of me died. Pain ripped through my body and tears formed rivers down my cheeks. *Someone save me.* The numbness crept into my mind and I let it pull me down into blissful nothingness. When he was done he rolled off of me and finally released his grip on my throat. I drew a ragged breath and lay silently in the darkness. He settled himself into the sleeping bag and after a short time, I heard his soft snores.

I stared at him from my corner of the tent, watching the slow rise and fall of his chest. *You could end it all right now.* My fingers itched with a twisted impulse. *No one is around to stop you... just kill him.* I inched closer to Christopher, feeling around as I went for some kind of weapon. The evil that usually clouded his face was gone and he looked almost normal. *A wolf in sheep's clothing.* The floor of the tent was smooth, cool, and wholly empty under my fingertips. I sighed deeply and crawled back to the furthest corner of the tent. As I stared at him, the thought of trying to crawl over him played at the edge of my mind. *You'll regret waking him up.* I remained rooted in place, terrified.

And so I sank down into the depths of my memories.

I could hear the screams from the other side of the door, and the smell of old pennies filled the air. Tears stung my eyes and I angrily wiped them away with the back of my hand. A stomach-turning wet splat sounded from the other side of the door and I gagged, vomit rushing into my mouth. I swallowed it down and pressed my back harder against the cool wood. *How had everything gotten this bad?* Something heavy crashed to the floor, and I winced.

"Help!" my mother's voice was shrill, fear the only distinguishable emotion in the word. I bowed my head, burying my face in my hands, and wished it was over. My jeans grew heavy with the river of blood that was flooding from beneath the door, staining me with my sins. I squeezed my eyes shut, frozen. Glass shattered and I jumped, closing my eyes tighter, burying my face further into my hands. Images of my parents' faces flashed behind my eyelids, their eyes wide with fear, their mouths hanging open as they realized what was happening... what I was doing. Tears stung my eyes and I tried to fight them off to no avail. *Monster.* The screams had turned into gurgles now. *Monster.* More blood came flooding in from beneath the door. *Monster.* What had I done? *How could you?*

I sat up, my muscles aching. I was alone. A new set of clothing was sitting in a small pile near the door along with a brush. I quickly changed clothes and ripped the brush through my hair. *You probably look like a tumbleweed.* I searched the tent again, hoping to find something in the morning light that I had missed last night, but I found nothing other than smears of my own blood. When I crawled outside, Christopher was still nowhere in sight. A bubble of hope rose in my chest. *Escape.* If I was fast enough, I could run and be gone before any of them even noticed.

Rachel caught my eye from the next tent over and she hurried over to me. "Christopher and Luke went out to check the traps. They'll be back soon, but I can help you get out of here now if you want." I studied her warily, searching for any indication that she was lying. She glanced around, scanning the camp. "We have to hurry if you want to get out. They won't be gone much longer." Trusting her was my only option and finally, I nodded.

"I don't know which way to go," I whispered.

She huffed and grabbed my hand, leading me towards the trees quickly. I looked around cautiously as we moved. The camp seemed empty, the tent doors blowing softly in the early morning breeze. *Where is everyone?* Once we were in the cover of the trees, she released my hand. "Go back to your group, then take them to the school. There's a whole town of survivors in this area."

"How do you know?" I asked, my eyes locking on her. *Safety.*

"I saw it written on one of the school walls, it's called Eden. It promised food and shelter to anyone that went to the gates. Go back to the school. There are directions on how to get there." *She saw it too.*

9

"Thank you. Why don't you come with me?" I reached for her hand, squeezing it tightly in mine.

She smiled almost sadly at me. "I still have business with Christopher."

"What happened with him?"

"Nothing you need to worry about," she said, pulling her hand from mine. "All you have to worry about is getting as far away from here as possible. They'll look for you when they realize you're gone. You have to get out of here."

"What if they find out you helped me? Won't they hurt you?"

"They can try." Her face was serious and I couldn't help but smile. Rachel was everything that I had ever wanted to be. "Now go." She shooed me forward.

"Thank you, Rachel."

She smiled at me as I moved further into the trees, picking my way through the thick underbrush. I stopped once she was out of sight. When I heard her head back toward the camp I followed, careful to stay low and quiet. She was risking everything for me, and I wasn't going to let them hurt her for it. *Stupid.* The tents came back into view and I crouched down in a bush not far from them, listening.

"Where is she?" It was Christopher's voice. "What do you mean you don't know?" I strained to hear Rachel's reply, but she was too far and too quiet. I tried to creep closer, tilting my head toward where they were to try and hear what she was saying. "I know you did something, Rachel. If I don't find her, you'll be replacing her."

10

Panic clawed its way into my brain as I replayed his threat, a broken tape recorder set on a loop. *She saved you... you can't let him hurt her.* I stood up before I could change my own mind. Christopher whirled to face me, his whole body vibrating with rage. Behind him, I could see Rachel; her lips pressed tight as she shook her head slowly before letting it drop. *What have you done?* When she lifted it again, her eyes narrowed, her fingers flexing. My chest tightened, nausea washing over me. *You screwed up.*

"Where were you?!" Christopher barked, stalking closer to me. His brown eyes were cold, the defined line of his jaw, hard. I took a tentative step back. "Where were you?!" He spat the words at me, pressing even closer. *Run.* I took another step back. *You had the chance to run and you fucked it up.* "Where?!" he roared. I stumbled over something and began to free-fall backward. *Rachel, help.* Before I could hit the ground, Christopher grabbed my arm and squeezed. He yanked me forward until I slammed into his broad chest. He smacked the side of my head with his hand, pinning my cheek to him as he leaned down to whisper, "You are going to wish that I killed you." *I already do.*

"Did you find any food, Sophia?" The barbed hint of a threat saturated the words. Christopher stiffened, casting a wary glance in her direction and letting me go.

"No," I said mechanically, taking a step back.

"That's alright," she said, stepping closer to Christopher. "Why don't I take you to get breakfast?" She focused her eyes on me, shifting from one foot to the other quickly. "Then we can go out together and look around."

10

"Okay." I tried to scoot around Christopher, but he moved with me, blocking Rachel from my view.

"That's alright Rachel." He waved a dismissive hand at her. "Luke and I wanted a chance to spend some time with Sophia." His lips stretched into a snarl. "But, could you take a look at Mara? She has a pretty nasty cut on her back."

"Another *accident?*" Rachel asked. I could hear the sarcasm dripping from her words.

He scoffed and waved her words away with the flick of his hand. "You know how clumsy she is." He said it as if the horrors that had happened to Mara by their hands were nothing but a childhood game of manhunt gone wrong. Rachel mumbled something I couldn't quite make out, dragging her hands through her hair and exhaling sharply before she crunched back through the leaves toward the tents. *Mara needs her more than you.* "Now," Christopher said. "Luke is waiting for you."

I crossed my arms defiantly, and glowered at Christopher, planting my feet firmly in the dirt. His eyes met mine and I deflated, though I tried to hide it. I wrapped my arms around my middle and quietly forced the words out. "I'm not a toy for you two to play with and break."

He was faster than I was prepared for. His fist smashed into my stomach and flung me back into the thorned branches of my long-lost sanctuary, the air bursting from my lungs in a startled yelp. He towered over me, sneering. "Rachel isn't here to protect you, little mouse." He grabbed the front of my shirt, the fibers tearing under the force, and hoisted me into the air as though I weighed no more than a doll. His face grew closer, hatred dripping from his eyes. I squirmed in his grasp, my clammy hands gripping his and squeezing until my knuckles turned white. "You will do as you are told." I flailed in his grasp, kicking and clawing at him in the hopes that he would drop me. *You should have run when you had the chance.* "Now. Luke is waiting for you. I promised him a turn." My stomach dropped and I went still in his hand, a rabbit cornered by the fox. No. As soon as he uncurled his fingers, I collapsed to the ground in a deflated heap. I didn't move. If I disobeyed enough, maybe he'd kill me out of frustration. *That would be too merciful for you.*

47

Images of Mara's empty gaze floated in my brain, swirling around and creating a home there. *A porcelain doll with a thousand little cracks.* The scars that decorated her skin told a horrible tale, but the ones that they had left in her mind were probably too terrifying for even her to recognize as scars anymore. Pain radiated through me as something hard collided with my abdomen. My arms wrapped reflexively around my middle as a second pain sliced through my back. I cried out again, shoving myself forward, struggling to crawl away from him as best I could with a hand still clutching my abdomen.

His dark laugh permeated my ears, "Big girls don't cry." *You aren't fast enough.*

"Why are you doing this to me?!" I yelled. I braced myself for the next hit, my arms instinctively raising to cover my head, but it didn't come. After a few seconds, I opened my eyes and looked into Christopher's face. His shoulders drooped, and the fire in his gaze seemed to dull, the spark snuffed out.

"Because he will do much worse." The words were barely a whisper, I almost didn't hear them. *What could be worse?* His eyes stared off into the distance, as though he was remembering something from long ago. I could have almost mistaken him as human at that moment. He didn't look like the same man that kidnapped and tortured me... almost like the mask had fallen away.

The snide retort that I had poised on the tip of my tongue withered as I studied the stranger suddenly before me. I let his words sink in. "What?" I whispered finally, tilting my head.

Anger instantly reignited in his eyes when he looked back at me, flint struck by a heavy stone. My heart thrashed in my ears, the trees feeling like they were closing in on me. I clenched my jaw as the world started spinning, my lungs aching from the shallow breaths I managed to suck down. He slammed his boot into my left thigh, knocking me on my side. I desperately tried to hoist myself to my feet, but his boot came down on me again, stomping on the arm still protecting my stomach. *This is what nightmares are made of.*

"This would be easier if you'd just listen," he quietly snarled through gritted

10

teeth. I nodded weakly but remained unmoving, still hoping for death. The metallic taste of blood coated my tongue and I swallowed it down, gagging. "Now get up, little mouse." Be good. Every part of my body cried out in pain as I struggled to my knees. I remained there shakily, the muscles in my thighs quivering as I fought back tears.

Christopher scoffed, crossing his arms and I forced myself to my feet. I wobbled unsteadily, swaying back and forth like a flower caught in a windstorm. "Good." There was less sharpness to his tone and I breathed an internal sigh of relief, hoping that meant I'd avoid another punishment. "Luke is probably wondering what I've done with you," he seethed. He turned his back on me and started walking. My muscles screamed at me to run, it was my chance to escape. *Don't be stupid.* My feet started moving, carrying me along behind him like a dog following its owner.

11

The Christopher I followed silently through the trees was different from the one that spent the last twenty-four hours tormenting me. He held branches out of the way for me and when I flinched at his touch, there was no roar in his voice, only an irritated mumble. *Even monsters play pretend.* Fear slowly flooded my system, and I grew more jittery with every passing second.

"Your brother," I began.

"Hm?" Christopher asked, holding a pine branch out of my path.

"He is going to hurt me worse than you did." It wasn't a question... I already knew the answer. I just wanted to hear him admit it.

"Probably." There was no emotion in his voice, no taunting. He may as well have been telling me the sky was blue. I think that scared me more.

"Why?"

He studied me, tilting his head slightly. "Don't ask questions you don't want the answer to." I opened my mouth but shut it again. *Don't poke the bear.* He wasn't hurting me, and I didn't want him to start again.

The rest of the walk was silent and I spent it contemplating my own stupidity. *You wasted your chance. You saved a girl that probably wasn't in any danger.*

"You're late." Luke's voice slithered under my skin as we entered a small clearing.

"There is no way to tell time Luke," Christopher sighed, his massive frame rising and falling as he ran his hand through his hair, pushing it back from his face. Luke shrugged and sauntered up to me, a huge smile painted on his face.

"Hello, Sophia," he purred, reaching a hand out to trace the cut on my cheek. I closed my eyes tightly. *Don't move.* His fingers were gentle as they probed and he made a clicking sound with his tongue. "It's a shame that such a pretty face has such a nasty cut. Why did you have to go and make me hurt you?"

I jerked, my eyes going wide. "W—what?"

His eyes softened and he reached to lightly tuck a strand of hair behind my ear, smiling sadly. "If you had just listened that wouldn't have happened."

"If you weren't a monster it wouldn't have either," I snapped, glaring at him.

His slap stung worse than Christopher's. The force broke the scab on my face open and blood poured down my cheek, dripping onto my shirt.

"Why can't you just listen, Sophia?"

I hated the sound of my name on his tongue, the way he tainted it. I pressed a shaking hand to my face, pulling it back to find my entire palm coated with crimson.

"This isn't my fault," I whispered. I glanced from Christopher with his shoulders hunched forward, to Luke and his dimpled grin. *A mouse caught in the claws of the cats.*

Luke circled me slowly, clicking his tongue the way a mother would to her disobedient child. "What are we going to do with you, Sophia?" He was faster than Christopher, arms ensnaring my waist before I realized he had even moved. He slammed me into his body and I screamed, flailing in his grasp. He crushed me, a laugh falling from his lips. He flashed a wicked smile before leaning in, his tongue touching the blood-soaked parts of my cheek.

He moaned and flattened his tongue against my skin, gripping me tighter. "You taste like heaven."

I couldn't help it this time; I heaved but nothing came out. *You haven't eaten in almost two days.* My stomach tightened, trying to expel something... anything. Acid burned my throat and I spat it out.

"Please," I begged. "Please leave me alone."

Luke's whole body shook with laughter. "Oh, Sophia." He patted my head gently, running his fingers through my hair. "I don't think that's possible." This time, the tears slid down my cheeks freely. Luke's fingers were feather light as he scooped one from my skin, touching it to his lip. The smear of liquid sat there for a moment before his tongue flicked out and licked it away. "What are we going to do with our precious Sophia, brother?" Luke asked, casting his eyes to Christopher.

Christopher shrugged, his expression bored. "I didn't even want to keep her. I don't really care what you do with her. Just don't leave a mess for me to clean up."

Luke scowled at his brother and rolled his eyes. When he looked back at me, he planted a wide grin on his face, the dimples in his cheeks making him look almost sweet. *Yeah, sweet like a rabid raccoon.* "We will just have to find something to entertain ourselves, Sophia." I wanted him to stop saying my name. It wasn't his to say. *Don't agitate him.*

His lips were soft when they touched my cheek and I flinched inwardly, squeezing my eyes shut tightly and wishing that I was back with Lucy and the others. He tightened his arms around my waist, pulling me harder against his body. He trailed kisses the length of my cheek and lingered close to my mouth. I clenched my teeth and squeezed my eyes shut tighter. He pressed his lips gently to mine and scoffed angrily when I refused to kiss him back. His tongue was greedy as it tried to invade my mouth. He snaked a hand up my body and wrapped it tightly around the front my throat.

"Look at me Sophia!" he barked. I drew a deep breath and opened my eyes. His piercing blue gaze burned me. "I saved you from my brother. You owe me at least one kiss."

Just do it. Don't make him mad. "No." *Dead girl.*

"What did you say to me?!" he roared. My whole body began to shake and the world started to spin as I sucked down shallow breaths, my heart thundering in my chest until it ached. I tried to pull away from him, pressing against his grip with all my weight. He flashed me a smug smile before opening his arms. I stumbled but managed to stay on my feet and tried to run. I took off in what I hoped was the direction Christopher and I had come from, a bubble of hope rising in my chest as the trees grew closer. *Only a few more steps and you're free.*

I was yanked back into reality, my freedom ripped away as I snagged myself on the protruding roots of a tree. The ground slammed into me and I rolled a few times. The world was spinning, and I thought that I would be sick again. I swallowed down the bile as Christopher's face floated into my line of vision. I blinked a few times, trying to focus on him and he leaned close to my face.

He pressed his lips to my ears, holding onto my shoulders. "Just do what he says, little mouse. It'll be less painful for you if you do." He hoisted me up, settling me on my feet. His hands lingered on my shoulders until I stopped swaying. When I looked into his face he seemed older than he had this morning. The wrinkles in his forehead were deeper, the lines in the corners of his eyes more pronounced. *Just do what he says.*

"Please bring her to me, Christopher. It's time to teach her some manners."

"Come on." Christopher nudged me forward and I bowed my head, my feet carrying me toward the executioner.

Luke wasn't gentle when he grabbed me this time. I winced at the bite of his fingers on my arm as he yanked me out of Christopher's grasp. Some sick part of me yearned for the sting of Christopher's hands instead. *At least Christopher stops.* Luke roughly positioned me so that I was standing in front of him, my back pressed to his front. My stomach lurched as he pushed against my back, the hard outline of his arousal rubbing on me as he moved his hips slowly. His hands wandered the front of my body, pinching and grabbing.

His lips touched the side of my neck, his breath searing my skin. "I'll make you scream for me this time, Sophia."

12

Tears streamed down my cheeks, dripping from my chin and falling onto Luke's roaming hands. He chuckled and pressed a soft kiss to the side of my neck, his teeth grazing the tender skin where my pulse fluttered erratically. I swallowed hard. "Don't cry, Sophia. I won't hurt you." *Liar.*

Christopher stood across from me, leaning against the large trunk of a tree. I searched his eyes for the mercy I hoped was buried in there. He stared back at me, the corners of his chocolate eyes crinkled slightly, his lips pressed in a thin line. *The lesser of two evils.*

Luke's fingers twisted in my hair and yanked my head back. He pressed his lips to my ear, whispering, "Does my brother turn you on?" Chills ran up and down my spine and I shook my head. "Then why," he yanked my head back harder, "are you looking at him?"

I clenched my teeth, biting down until I was sure that they would shatter. My scalp screamed in agony and adrenaline surged through me. "Let go!" I screamed trying to rip myself out of his grasp.

He tightened his grip. "Stop making me hurt you, Sophia." He rested his chin on my shoulder, his breath hot and wet against the bare skin of my neck.

I froze.

His teeth scraped my skin again and I sucked in a quiet gasp. Memories of his teeth sinking into the tender spot on my shoulder assaulted me, smashing into me over and over. *Please no.* He bit down hard and I dropped my shoulder, trying to angle myself away from him. Blood dripped down my neck, soaking into the collar and sleeve of my shirt. I cried out as he pushed his teeth further into my skin. The trickle of blood grew to a river and I squirmed in his grasp, trying to rip myself free. *Monster.* More tears poured down my face and I couldn't help the scream that burst from me in sheer desperation. I sunk my nails into his arm, digging them deep enough to feel blood pool out around them. My head was swimming. I felt like I was floating in a pool of water. My stomach lurched and the edges of my vision began to grow blurry. *There's so much blood.*

"Luke," Christopher warned. My eyelids fluttered as I tried to force them to stay open. "Lucas!" he roared. Everything went out of focus. *Don't lose sight of them.* I fought the unconsciousness, teetering on the edge, ready to fall into the dark abyss. *Stay awake.* I tried to concentrate on Christopher's large frame. *What's he doing?* He slammed into us, sending Luke and I sprawling onto the ground. As we fell, Luke finally stopped biting me and I lay quietly in the grass, blood leaking from the fresh wound and sinking into the dirt.

"What the fuck Christopher?!" Luke growled. I tried to turn my head to look at them, but nausea kept me still.

"Why did you bite her like that?!" Christopher snapped.

"Because I like the way she tastes!"

"What the hell is wrong with you?" Christopher's voice was quiet when he said it, as if he were afraid of what his brother's answer might be.

"Nothing," Luke growled.

Silence settled around me as I fought to stay awake, more and more of my blood slowly draining from the bite in my neck. Everything grew cold and my limbs felt heavy. *Just go to sleep. It's time to stop fighting.* Images of Lucy, Jax, and Mason drifted in and out of focus in front of me. *They'll be alright without you.*

"Are you insane?" It was Christopher's voice. Jax's smile sent a surge of sadness through me. *Lucy will protect her.* I could almost hear her laugh. *Mason will protect her.*

"No," Luke sighed. More of my blood poured out around me, permeating the air with the scent of pennies.

"Are you trying to get us killed? Look at all the fucking blood, Luke!" There was a desperation in Christopher's voice that shocked me even through the fog. He was afraid. *The big bad wolf is afraid of something.*

"So what? You didn't even want her. We can just leave her here and let those things have her." *Please let me die before then.*

"We can't go back without her, Luke."

"Why not? Just tell everyone she ran off."

"Rachel will kill me if I don't come back with her! She almost killed me when I didn't come back with Katie!" *Who's Katie?*

The hair on the back of my neck stood up and my blood went cold. *There's no noise.* The chirping of the birds had stopped and in the distance, something heavy stepped on a branch, snapping it. I opened my mouth to try to warn them but no sound came out. *You are going to die. They are going to leave you to die.* Another snap sounded in the still air, closer this time. I sighed inwardly and closed my eyes, resigning myself to death. It was coming whether I liked it or not.

Low, predatory growls penetrated the humid summer air and I drew a deep breath.

"What was that?" Luke asked.

"It was us," a strange voice whispered from the shadows between the trees directly in front of me.

"Shit." Christopher's voice sounded panicked. *At least he will die afraid too.*

"We've got to go," Luke urged.

"We can't leave her here. Rachel will have my head."

"She's bleeding all over Christopher."

"Who's fucking fault is that?!" Christopher barked.

Another growl came from the trees and one of the shadows moved, coming out into the sunlight. Blood dripped from the corners of its mouth, and it smiled with half-rotten teeth. I wanted to scream, but I didn't have the energy to. Two more shadows moved and ventured into the daylight. *No one is making it out of this meadow alive.*

"What do we do?" Luke asked.

"Die," one of the things giggled. It flashed a gap-toothed grin and stalked forward, its bloodshot eyes locked on me. *You can't even try to save yourself.*

"You can have her, just let us go," Luke begged. *Asshole.*

"Lucas!" Christopher hissed. "She has to come with me!" *Maybe it would be better if he left you to die.*

"We don't make bargains," one of the shredders rasped. There was something unsettling about their voices; the way they rasped out the words as though they were suffocating and couldn't get enough air. I closed my eyes tightly as the shredder got closer, its mouth open wide, ready to rip into my skin the way Luke had done moments ago. *Maybe this torture will end faster.*

Hands grabbed me and I swallowed my scream, bracing myself for the pain that was coming for me like an out-of-control train. My eyes flew open, as I was dragged back from my oncoming death, the grass scrapping at my skin, my blood leaving a thick trail in the dirt. Christopher stepped over me, blocking out the shredders. *He's protecting you.* My muddled brain tried to connect the puzzle to understand what was happening, but it seemed that I was missing a few important pieces. Luke appeared beside his brother, something silver flashing in his hands. *A knife.* Christopher lunged forward quickly before dancing back, from the reaching claws aimed for his skin.

"When can we leave her and run?" Luke asked, striking at one of the things.

Christopher looked at him for only a second before taking another swing at one of the shredders. It fell onto the grass, eyes opened wide, the knife stuck to the hilt in the side of its head.

"Just let the goddamn things have her and we'll bring the pieces back for Rachel!" Luke yelled, jumping back from a set of snapping teeth.

"Shut up Luke!" Christopher sneered. "You're going to get us both killed if you don't shut up!" *Was Christopher that afraid of Rachel?*

"I'll help," I whispered dazedly. I pressed my palms into the blood-stained grass and tried to hoist myself up on shaking arms. I only made it a few inches before my muscles gave out and I collapsed back into the growing puddle of scarlet.

Christopher looked back at me, his eyes wide with fear, his face spattered with dozens of too dark blood droplets. "Don't move!" he growled. *No problem.*

"She's dying anyway, Christopher. Why can't we just leave her?" Luke's knife made contact with the second shredder, sinking deep into its eye socket. Luke twisted the blade and there was a sickening crunch.

"Because I fucking said so, Luke!" Christopher's whole body was shaking but I wasn't sure if it was from rage or fear. He lunged at a shredder, a bloody smacking sound ripping through the meadow. The body crumpled to the grass, Christopher on top of it. His fists connected again and again with the thing's head, blood spraying up and drenching the entire front of him.

It was rage. But at least it isn't directed at you this time.

13

Christopher finally climbed off the shredder, blood dripping from his hair, he ran his hands through it, pushing it back from his face. The blood formed thick rivers running down his face and dripping onto his shirt from his chin. His shadowed eyes fell on me and he sauntered over, kneeling down in my blood. He was gentle when he touched my cheek, gingerly turning my head and frowning deeply as he examined the bite on my neck.

"I won't let the monster get you, little mouse."

"Which one?" I whispered. I braced myself for a hit, but he simply rolled his eyes and slid his arms under me. He lifted me as though I was weightless and settled me against his chest, one arm under my knees, the other across my back.

I tried to keep my head up but didn't have the strength and I laid it against him, listening to the beating of his heart and the rumbling of his voice when he spoke. "Let's go Luke."

The walk back was short, my foggy brain drifting in and out of consciousness. The darkness threatened to swallow me, pulling me down into its depths and keeping me captive there.

"Oh my god! What happened to her?!" Rachel's voice pulled me back to the light. My eyelids were heavy as I opened them and tried to turn my head. "Why is there so much blood?"

"There was an incident," Christopher rumbled.

"What kind of incident?" Rachel sneered.

"It's not important Rachel!" Christopher barked. "You just need to fix it!"

"Is that a bite mark?" Rachel seethed. I managed to turn my head and was met with her horrified eyes darting between Christopher's face and mine.

"No," Luke purred.

Rachel looked at him and narrowed her eyes before sighing, "Bring her into my tent."

Christopher followed along behind Rachel and I settled my head back against his chest, closing my eyes. *Maybe you're already too far gone.*

"Put her down over there and get out." Her voice was cold. Christopher's warmth vanished, replaced by the cool tent floor. I heard the tent zip closed and tried to open my eyes again. Rachel's face floated in and out of focus. "What did he do to you?" she whispered, touching my cheek softly.

"Luke," I rasped softly.

"Luke?" she questioned. "What about him? Did he do this to you?" I tried to nod, but the darkness was trying to pull me down again. I closed my eyes and let it swallow me.

Everything was silent on the other side of the closet door and I lifted my head, wiping the tears from my cheeks with the back of my hand. I got onto my knees and reached for the doorknob, turning it with a soft click. *Murderer.* The coppery stench of blood hung thick in the air, suffocating me as it consumed my senses. The door swung open.

Horror greeted me.

Smears of blood adorned the once-white walls, the macabre mural forever immortalizing what I'd done. I took a shaky step into the room, my knees almost buckling. My feet splashed in the still-warm puddles on the floor. The liquid seeped between my toes and bile rose in my throat, burning as I swallowed it back down. I refused to look anywhere but the wide open door. Slowly, I made my way toward it, dragging the soles of my feet across the nail-gouged floor. My foot hit something large and against my better judgment, I looked down.

I choked back the scream that pressed against the inside of my lips. My eyes focused on the paper airplane tattoo on the waxy skin, the delicate black lines ripped apart with droplets of blood. *Mom was so proud of that tattoo.* My eyes drifted upward and I couldn't stop the vomit as I stumbled back. Bits of shredded flesh clung to the severed leg, hanging limply from the massive wound. I fell backward and splashed into a large puddle of blood, my hands slipping out from under me. My head bounced off the floor and I lay there quietly with my eyes closed, praying for it all to go away. *Count to three and open your eyes.* I rolled to my stomach and took a deep breath. *One.* I placed my palms on the floor. *Two.* I clenched my teeth. *Three.* I screamed.

The underside of the bed greeted me, the shadows reaching out for me. My gaze focused on the severed head of my father, his mouth open in a silent scream, his eyes wide with fear. *It's all your fault.* This time the bile poured past my lips, my stomach convulsing painfully until it was empty. I staggered to my feet. Tears poured down my cheeks, mixing with the blood and vomit. Everywhere I looked, there was another body part. The room began to spin and I stumbled on unsteady feet toward the door, desperate to escape.

I could barely see through the tears as I staggered into the hallway toward my bedroom. The door was ajar and I pushed it open, heading for the dresser and ripping new clothes from the drawers. I stripped my blood-drenched clothing off and let it fall to the floor with a sickening splat. *Wash the blood off, stupid.* I ran past my parents' open door and didn't stop until I slammed the bathroom door behind me. The water was cold, and I shivered under the stream as I scrubbed my skin until it was raw. *It will never come off.* I climbed out, wrapping myself in a thick towel that smelled like my mom. *You are stained forever by what you've done.* I choked on a sob and rubbed my body with the towel until it burned from the force, desperate to hold on to the scent. I didn't look in the mirror as I left the room, afraid of the person who would be looking back at me. On my way out the door, I slid my boots on and grabbed my mother's navy blue jacket from the hook in the entryway.

"Sophia?" Rachel's voice wrapped around me like a warm blanket. "Sophia wake up." My lids still felt heavy and I fought to open them. Rachel's caramel eyes were wide, focused on my face under brows that were knit together. "I thought you were going to die," she whispered, pushing my hair back from my face.

"I still might," I croaked.

"Don't say that!" she scolded softly. She glared at me, but her expression soon softened and she offered me a small smile. "You're definitely a fighter."

"Rachel?" I asked.
"Hmm?"
"Who's Katie?"

14

Tension hung thick enough to cut it, pressing down on us in the silence of the tent.

She broke it first. "She was my sister."

"What happened to her?"

She took a deep breath, wrapping her arms around her middle and staring blankly at the far wall of the tent, the corner of her lips turning down in a hard frown. "She died." She took a deep breath through her nose and held it for a few seconds before continuing. "She was my entire world. My parents died before all this really started, so it was just Katie and I. Once everything went to shit, we headed into the mountains to try to stay safe. She was only a few years younger than me, but my parents sheltered and spoiled her... she was the baby after all." I could hear the smile in her voice and she lifted a shaking hand to brush the hair out of her face. "She was such a ray of sunshine. She always tried to see the best in people, even when there was nothing good to find." *Just like Jax.* Rachel chewed the inside of her cheek and her hands dropped into her lap, her eyes following. She cupped one hand in the other and squeezed. "I tried my best to keep her away from other people. When we found Michael, I was wary, but the group was bigger then. Plus it was full of families so I thought it would be safe.

"Christopher and Luke were already part of the group, but it was easy to avoid them. They were busy chasing the other girls around," Rachel bit out, her words dripping with disgust. "When our group started to dwindle, that's when they noticed Katie." She swallowed hard and she glared at the floor. "I never liked them. They always stared after her like a pair of hungry wolves.

When Christopher started asking for her help with different camp chores, I tried to tell her no, but she insisted. She promised me that she'd be careful, even though she couldn't see how they were dangerous. She treated them like injured birds, fawning over them and thinking she could heal the broken parts they showed her. She told me once that they were just a little rough around the edges and they just needed kindness. She believed that so deeply that she couldn't see they were poison."

Her voice cracked and she drew a shaky breath. "I woke up one morning and she was gone. Michael told me Christopher asked her to go get firewood with him and Luke. They came back in the late afternoon, but she wasn't with them. I asked them where she was and they told me she had gotten scared by some loud noises in the forest and headed back to camp hours ago. They pretended to be worried. They even helped look for her." She took another breath, letting it out slowly. "I was the one that found her. She was just laying there in a field. She looked so peaceful. I thought she was sleeping at first."

Her hands squeezed into fists in her lap and she hissed through gritted teeth. "But when I yelled her name, she didn't move." Her whole body shook. "When I got closer, I could tell her clothes were torn to shreds. And then I saw the bruises." Rachel's eyes finally met mine for the first time since she started talking and she leaned in. I wasn't even sure she was blinking as her eyes burned into mine. She spoke each word slowly and low, a dark secret drenched in anguish and hatred. "They were handprints. All of them. Huge purple and black and blue splotches... including the ones circling her throat. I grabbed her hand and there was blood caked under her nails... she tried to fight."

She paused and swept the tears from her face, never breaking eye contact. "I could never prove it, but I knew it was them. They took her from me and then had the audacity to stand at her grave and cry when I buried her." Her face reddened and she gulped down strained breath after strained breath. "Christopher has a scar," she whispered. "It's on the right side of his chest. I saw it once when he took his shirt off." She closed her eyes and took another breath. "It's a scratch mark."

I couldn't think of the words to say. 'I'm sorry' wasn't enough to acknowledge such a significant loss. "I wish I could bring her back for you."

Rachel offered me the ghost of a smile before whispering, "So do I."

Silence settled itself between us, falling too easily into a conversation where it spoke more about what Rachel said than either of us could. Eventually, Rachel sighed and reached over to pick up a small glass vial. She turned it over slowly in her hands before getting up and taking it to the trunk by the door of the tent. "What happened to you today Sophia?" She didn't look at me.

The memory was fuzzy. *It's probably better that way.* "I remember Christopher being nice to me. And I remember something biting me, there was so much blood." The sickening, ghostly memory of hands groping my body made me wince. I shivered sucking air through my clenched teeth at the sharp pain in my shoulder and neck.

"Try not to move too much," Rachel soothed, her cool fingers touching the fevered skin of my face. "What bit you?"

I managed a joyless chuckle. "Not a shredder."

Rachel didn't seem to find any humor in my statement and turned to scowl at me. "Sophia."

I sighed, grimacing at the pain in my sides and ribs. "Will telling you change anything?"

"What do you mean?"

"Will it make it so it never happened? Will it save me from it happening again?" Anger bubbled inside my chest. *How could you be so weak? Why didn't you fight harder?*

Rachel bit her lip and sighed. "It was Christopher wasn't it?"

I shook my head.

Rachel cocked her head and her eyes widened slightly. "Luke?"

"Who else?" I mumbled, lifting my hand to gingerly poke at the wound on my neck. My fingers touched the edges of the strings holding the skin together. "Did you stitch this?"

"Why would Luke bite you?" she demanded sitting back down in front of me.

"Because he's a monster," I grumbled, still touching the stitches. "Why did you stitch this? Won't it get infected?"

"Are you sure it wasn't Christopher?" Her eyes were wide, boring into mine as she leaned forward.

"I think I know whose teeth were in my neck, Rachel!" I barked. She jerked at my tone and crossed her arms. "Now, why did you stitch a bite closed?"

"Because you were bleeding to death," she hissed. "The risk of infection is low in that area because of the blood flow." She threw her arms up and angled her body away from me.

We fell into silence once more. After a few minutes, I opened my mouth to speak, but Christopher's voice broke the silence first. "Is she alive?" His shadow loomed across the wall of the tent as he hovered outside the door. "Rachel?"

Rachel reached over and yanked the zipper open, revealing a very irritated Christopher. My heart skipped a beat and I clenched my hands into fists. "What do you want?" she bit out.

"Is she alright?"

"Why do you care? She was almost dead when you brought her to me." She took a step toward him, craning her neck to stare into his face.

His broad shoulders rose and fell with a deep sigh. "Can I take her to my tent now?"

"No!" Rachel snarled.

He recoiled from her as though she had struck him. Dozens of emotions flashed in his gaze before the ice returned and he straightened his back, rising to his full height and towering over Rachel. "I am taking her with me Rachel," he rumbled, low and menacing.

Rachel squared her shoulders, her jaw clenching. "No, you aren't." She jabbed a finger at him. "Now go away."

"No."

Rachel froze and tilted her head as the word tumbled off Christopher's tongue. "What?"

"Give her to me, Rachel. You don't have enough space in there for the both of you. All your equipment is in the way. I don't even know how you sleep

14

in there. She'll be more comfortable where she can spread out."

I glanced around Rachel's tent, realizing for the first time how crowded it really was. Her large trunk of medical supplies took up almost half the space, a backpack and smaller gray box taking up another quarter of what was left.

"What she needs is to be away from you and your psycho brother," Rachel sneered.

Christopher's face reddened, his hands clenching into tight fists at his sides. *Danger.* If Rachel noticed, she didn't seem to care. She didn't budge from the doorway of the tent, blocking his entrance. *He'll kill her.*

"Rachel," I whispered. "I'll go with him." *Always sacrificing yourself for someone else.*

15

Rachel narrowed her eyes at me, her head flinched back slightly. I mustered a smile. "It'll be alright. You need your space to rest." I forced myself up to a sitting position. "I have a feeling Mara might have another accident soon," I whispered, trying to keep my voice too low for Christopher to hear.

Rachel raised a brow at me before narrowing her eyes at Christopher. "Be careful with her. She needs to rest. She lost a lot of blood."

Christopher mumbled an acknowledgment and Rachel frowned as she finally stepped aside, pressing her back against the tent wall so there was a small space for Christopher to step inside. His massive frame engulfed the scant free space, and the tent felt impossibly more cramped.

"Can you walk?" he asked, rolling his eyes. *Jerk.*

I looked to Rachel for an answer. She frowned but nodded. "Yeah," I mumbled, bracing myself for the pain that would come from having to stand up. I focused on the ground as I struggled to get to my feet. Christopher's hand appeared in my line of sight. I paused and looked up at him.

His face was blank, all the lines smoothed out and I squinted at him. *He doesn't even look like the same person.* He offered me his hand.

He noticed me staring at him and stiffened. "Just take my help," he grumbled.

Don't let him know you're weak. I began to force myself to let him take my hand, only to falter a couple seconds later, my hand frozen in mid-air. I needed someone to help me stand. I didn't want to have to struggle and hurt in the name of dignity. *Not that you have much of that left anyway.* Finally, I surrendered, putting my hand in his. My heart jumped at the soft skin that touched mine. *These can't be the same hands that left a torrent of bruises on you.* He tugged me to my feet. All of my muscles screamed as I was brought to my feet. My head spun and nausea ripped through me as I teetered unsteadily. The tent began to spin and I clutched at Christopher's hand tighter, holding on with all my strength. *Weak.*

He huffed and mumbled something under his breath, squaring his shoulders and squeezing my hand tighter. My fingers cracked as he invaded my space. *You let your guard down.* I tried to pull my hand back, but he held it even tighter, my bones groaning as he started to crush them. *You're trapped now.* I shrunk away from him, the pain and desperation not enough to dull the fear that he stirred in me. I was small and fragile beside him, and I had to crane my neck to look up into the bottomless pit of his eyes. Their darkness threatened to consume me as he reached to grab more of me. I tried to swallow the growing lump in my throat as he hauled me into his arms, gripping my waist and legs painfully.

I jerked my head to look at Rachel, begging her to let me stay, regretting my decision to leave already. She crossed her arms as she glowered at Christopher.

"Thank you, Rachel," he whispered before stepping into the night.

The air was cooler than it had been the past few months. I took a deep breath of it, letting it fill my lungs and wash through me. *Fall will be here soon.* I tilted my chin up, staring up at the cloudless night sky. Thousands of stars shimmered overhead; glitter splashed across the darkness. *How long did you sleep?*

"Christopher!" Luke's voice sent ice shooting through my veins and I curled reflexively into Christopher. *The lesser of two evils.*

Christopher stopped walking. "What?" he hissed.

"I see Sophia is alive."

"Yeah," Christopher grumbled.

"You can drop her off in my tent. Mara can stay with you tonight."

"Are you fucking insane?" Christopher snapped. I cringed at the venom in his voice. "You know what," he continued. "Don't answer that. I already know the answer." He started to turn away and I relaxed a little. *Stupid.*

SURVIVOR

"What's your fucking problem?" Luke growled.

Christopher paused, only turning his head. "You," he said coolly.

"*Me?!*" Luke roared.

Christopher took a deep breath, his chest pushing against me as he did so. "Yes," he said, breathing out heavily. "Now leave me alone. I don't want to deal with you right now." He continued walking, ignoring his brother as Luke yelled his name. Won't the others notice? His mood seemed to have shifted, his muscles tighter than they had been when we left the tent, the tension clear in his jaw.

The walk to his tent was too short. He stood in front of the zipped door, staring at it like a puzzle that needed to be solved. *He can't unzip it while he's holding you.*

"You can put me down," I whispered.

He nodded and gingerly set me on my feet, his hands resting on my hips until I stopped swaying. My legs felt like jelly, quivering with the energy that it took to keep me upright. When the tent door fell open I took a step toward it and almost fell on my face.

"For fuck's sake," Christopher huffed. "Let me help you before you hurt yourself."

"It's fine," I mumbled, trying to take another step. The world spun out of control and the ground started coming toward my face. I blearily tried to catch myself but my arms gave out. I fell flat on my stomach, my forehead smacking off the hard dirt.

"Yeah," he grumbled. "You're definitely fine." He stepped over me into the tent and plopped down on his sleeping bag, staring at me with a wry smile. "Come on, little mouse. You said you could do it. So do it." *He's going to make you beg for his help.*

I glowered at him, struggling to get on my hands and knees, my stomach churning. Pain throbbed through my head with every beat of my heart and I gagged, bile burning my throat. I spat it into the dirt, the bitter taste coating my tongue and triggering another bout of heaving.

"You're doing a great job," Christopher yawned. I lifted my head to glare at him, a thousand vile words sitting on the tip of my tongue; ready to be unleashed on the beast lounging comfortably among his pillows and blankets. A snarky smile curled his lips up, his white teeth flashing at me as he laughed. "You gonna ask for help yet?" *No.*

I shook my head and started to crawl forward, swallowing hard to keep the acid down. Every movement was agony. Once I was completely inside I collapsed onto the cool tent floor, pressing my fevered face to the smooth fabric. Sweat beaded on my forehead despite the chill in the air. Golden light flashed out of the corner of my eye and I glanced at Christopher. The candle he held in his hand was half spent, large trails of wax creeping down the side of it.

"You should eat something before you go to sleep," Christopher said, rummaging around in the dirty blue backpack leaning against the wall near the door. Eventually, he dug out a granola bar and tossed it at me, smacking me in the head with it. It hurt more than it should have, but I bit my tongue. *Don't show him your weakness.*

"Thanks," I mumbled, trying to sit up.

"Are you gonna ask for help yet?" There was no malice in his tone when he asked.

I shook my head, ever defiant. "No."

"Suit yourself," he said, snuffing out the candle and snuggling down into his sleeping bag.

I lay perfectly still in the darkness, taking a few deep breaths and allowing my body a chance to relax. After the ache in my muscles faded a bit, I took a deep breath, holding it as I pushed myself up into a sitting position. Tears stung my eyes and I rapidly blinked them away. In the darkness, I fumbled blindly for the granola bar, my fingers gliding across the tent floor slowly. My stomach growled at the thought of food and I smiled to myself when my fingertips bumped into the smooth plastic wrapper. I hungrily tore it open and stuffed the first bite into my mouth greedily. A small moan escaped my lips and my face grew hot with embarrassment.

I heard Christopher chuckle in the darkness, and then something warm and soft landed half in my lap. I touched it, running my hands across the minky fabric. *A blanket.* I stared at the space that I knew he occupied quietly.

Why is he being so nice? Tentatively, I wrapped the warm fabric around my body, shoving the last of the granola bar into my mouth. *It's probably a trick.*

16

Luke's icy gaze consumed my nightmares. His voice sliced deep into my brain, ripping out the happy memories and settling itself among the newfound shadows. The places that his fingers touched me still burned, the bruised skin a reminder of the darkness he had infected me with. *Death would be better than Luke.*

When the world came into focus the next morning, Christopher was gone. I rubbed a hand down my face and forced myself to sit up. Everything hurt worse than it had last night. *How is that even possible?* Beside me was another granola bar and a bottle of water. *He's being too nice.* I shrugged off the eerie feeling that settled in my stomach and stuffed the granola bar into my mouth before using the water to wash it down. I hadn't realized how thirsty I was.

I froze as the zipper on the tent suddenly began to open. My heart sped up, pounding in my chest at the thought of his hands touching my skin again.

Two empty hazel orbs peered at me from the half-open door, short tendrils of wavy brown hair framing a heart-shaped face.

"Mara?" I asked softly. A sheepish smile touched her delicate pink lips and she unzipped the door just a little more, slipping inside and hurriedly zipping it closed again. She turned her head to me slowly and I sucked in a breath in through my teeth. Mara was beautiful in a way that I had only dreamed of being when I was younger. Her smooth olive skin was dotted with a few dark freckles, and her large doe-like eyes were framed by thick dark lashes. The longer I studied her, the more noticeable the broken pieces left behind by the brothers became. Deep purple splotches covered her arms and throat. Older sickly yellow-green ones dotted across her cheekbones disappeared at her hairline. Large jagged scars marred almost every part of her skin that was visible. The largest one was right in the center of her chest, nestled between her collarbones. My breath caught painfully in my chest. An ugly, jagged 'L' was carved there.

"Look what he did to you," she whispered. Her voice was flat and empty... as if all the emotion had been ripped out of her. *They destroyed her.*

"Look at what they did to *you*," I countered.

Her face reddened and she dropped her eyes to the floor. "I'm clumsy," she mumbled, picking at the skin around her thumbnail.

"Mara," I urged. "I know it was them."

She shook her head, her brown ringlets bouncing. "It was just an accident. I fall a lot." She was like a trained dog. The broken girl in front of me tugged at my heart. When she looked at me, it was like looking at a doll. Her lovely hazel eyes swirled with oceans of blue and vast meadows of green... but they were void of anything, absent of the life that had once called the beautiful shell its home. *Will you ever come back, Mara? Are you still in there?*

"Do you need help, Mara?"

She shook her head again and bit her bottom lip. "You do."

"What do you mean?"

"You don't have to be stuck here. You have a group looking for you. You have someone who misses you."

"I don't even know if they are looking for me."

"You have to try," she pleaded.

"They won't let me leave," I growled. I took a steadying breath. "I tried yesterday."

She frowned at me. "Rachel told me that she got you out... and that you came back." For the first time, I could almost hear something in her voice, the faintest twinge of anger lacing itself through her words.

My face reddened. "Yeah," I whispered. "I did."

"This time," she began, "this time you can't come back." Before the gravity of her words could fully sink in, she was moving. She pulled the zipper of the tent and peeked out. "Come on," she whispered, unzipping it just enough to slip out. I groaned and forced myself up, following her.

The sunlight was blinding. Mara was fast, and I rushed to keep up with her, squinting and shading my eyes with my hand to try to see. The toe of my boot snagged on a tent spike and I reflexively tried to keep myself from falling by grabbing Mara. *Shit.*

She stumbled and we both crashed to the dirt in a cloud of swear words and shattered hope.

"Come on Sophia." Before I could fully comprehend what was going on, Mara was back on her feet, bouncing from one foot to the other, her eyes scanning the camp. "Hurry."

"I'm trying," I rasped, fumbling to get up, my entire body screaming in agony.

The treeline was almost within reach when Luke's voice roared from behind, a noose reaching out for the both of us. "Mara!"

Fear gripped me in its stranglehold, squeezing until the edges of my vision grew fuzzy and dim. Mara refused to stop, grabbing my hand and towing behind her as I suffocated.

"Mara!" he barked out again. I could only imagine the rage rolling off of him, the hatred boiling in his blue eyes. I opened my mouth in a silent scream, tears rolling past my lips, their bitter taste like ashes on my tongue. *She's just as scared as you are.*

Mara's hand shook in mine, as she held me tighter, like a lifeline. "Come on, Sophia. We're almost there."

I tried desperately to keep my footing as we ran into the trees, disappearing amongst the leaves and branches.

"Mara!"

Mara dragged me behind a large thorny bush, crouching down and looking into my face. "Run Sophia," she panted. "Count to three and then run. I'll try to lead him away."

I grabbed her hand with both of mine, holding her tightly. "Come with me. You can get away from them."

For a second, something flickered in her eyes. *Hope.* It was gone as quickly as it had come, the nothingness consuming her again, and she shook her head. "I can't," she whispered. "Someone has to distract them."

All I could do was nod. She untangled herself from my grasp and crept a few feet away from me. Her small frame rose and fell as she drew a deep breath and popped up to full height. She stood for a moment, a deer in the headlights, before taking off in the opposite direction.

"One," I whispered, peaking through the branches of the bush, searching for him. "Two." I steadied myself on my feet, breathing through the pain that seared through my entire body. "Three."

I ran, begging my legs to carry me faster. The green blur of trees flew past my face as I narrowly avoided collision after collision. I ran blindly, with no clue where I was going, only that it was very far away from Christopher and Luke. *Safety.*

17

By the time I stopped running, my muscles were screaming in agony. I doubled over, pressing my back against the trunk of a tree as I dry heaved. The adrenaline began to ebb from my system, and my legs started to shake. I slowly sank until my thighs touched the damp earth. I lay my head back and closed my eyes, listening to the sounds of the forest around me.

"I think she went this way!" I went cold at the sound of his voice. I pushed myself harder against the tree and looked around, straining to see him through the thick undergrowth. *Dear God, don't let them find me.* As I sat in silence, I could make out the sound of their footfall, twigs and leaves screaming under their boots.

"Are you sure?"

"Yes."

I couldn't tell who was speaking, but with each second they were getting closer.

"When I find her, she's gonna wish we'd killed her."

"What about Mara?"

"What about her? I knew she left the little bitch behind when I saw her take off." He'd known it was a trick. He must have been following me the whole time. *Stupid girl.*

I tried to make myself smaller, tucking my legs close to my body. *How didn't you hear them?* Everything hurt, the dull ache rising to a screaming pain in my limbs and head. Sweat rolled down the side of my neck, settling in the stitches. The salt burned the fresh wound. Leaves and pine needles crunched under their feet. *They're so close.* I held my breath, hoping they would go away. The footsteps stopped. *They're going to find you.* There was silence and I covered my mouth with my hands to mask the breath I had to draw. There were no more footsteps, no more voices. *Maybe they went away.*

"Gotcha!" I let out a high-pitched wail and flailed to slide away from him. In a scene straight out of my nightmares, he reached out toward me, his glacier-blue eyes chilling me to my core. His mouth opened wide, white teeth flashing in the shadow of bushes, and a laugh tumbled out as I scrambled through the carpet of branches and pine needles.

I got to my feet and started to run, smashing into Christopher before I even had a chance. "Where do you think you're going?" I tried to push him away, but his arms encircled me like a snare. "You really thought that you were going to get away, didn't you little mouse?"

"Just let me go." I choked on the words as they tumbled out, pleading with the devil, knowing that monsters don't bargain.

"Why would we do that?" Luke's face floated into my line of vision, his lips twisting into a humorless sneer. I felt the fight slowly leaving my body, apathy finding a home within the broken parts of me. This was karma for what I'd done... karma for the sacrifice I chose to make. The hope for freedom, and the drive to escape all came crumbling down around me, collapsing in on themselves and threatening to crush me in the falling ruble.

"Giving up already, little mouse?" His body rumbled against mine as he taunted me. *The Christopher that gave you a blanket and a granola bar is gone.* Instead of answering, I stared off into the distant trees, counting the leaves like the minutes left in my life. I felt myself crumpling to the ground. I pulled my knees to my chest and lay as still as I could, hoping they would get it over with quickly. The sharp jab to my back had me hissing a breath through my gritted teeth but I remained unmoving, still staring into the shadows of the trees. A branch shifted slightly and Lucy's face came into focus. She stared at me for a moment before pressing her finger to her lips and slowly letting the branch go until she was hidden from view.

My stomach tightened involuntarily. *She came looking for you.* A new fear drilled itself into my brain, making a hole there. What if he saw her? What if he *and* his brother saw her and went after her? What if they found Jax? Jax had to be close, Lucy would never let her and Mason stray too far. Mason was large and his size alone might be enough to deter one of the brothers, but not for long, not once they realized that he wasn't truly a threat to them.

"Get up. We have to get back." *Back?* The sickening realization hit me like a speeding truck. They didn't intend to make my death a quick one. I stood slowly, still staring into the treeline. His hands were in my hair and he shoved me forward, almost sending me face-first into the dirt. "Walk."

The branch where Lucy had been twitched again and I could almost see the look of disapproval that was painted on her face, though it remained hidden among the leaves. Lucy would have never let this happen to herself. She would have fought tooth and nail until they either killed her or she had gotten away. And yet, here I was, beaten and being dragged around like a dog. Anger boiled inside of me. How had I allowed myself to be diminished to this? How had I so quickly decided to lie down and die?

"I'm not a dog." The words were calculated. They would make him mad. They would earn me another punishment but I didn't care.

He snagged my hair, pulling until tears stung my eyes. "You," his face drew close to my ear, "are," his lips touched my skin, "whatever I," his free hand slithered until it rested on my throat, "say." He squeezed, the pressure making the edges of my vision grow fuzzy. Blood ran down my neck, my stitches opening up. My lungs burned and I clawed at his fingers, desperately trying to pull them loose. The haze began to claim more of my vision and adrenaline surged wildly through my body.

Fight. My nails dug deeper into his fingers. *Fight.* I leaned back into him, desperate to try and get any ounce of air, to drive the haze from my vision. I kicked, trying to gain enough momentum to throw him off balance. He squeezed harder, and I felt the life beginning to leave. My foggy brain reached deep into itself, searching wildly for anything to save itself from my stupidity. I went limp, allowing my full weight to sag onto him. After another agonizing heartbeat, his grip loosened. When I remained unmoving he let me go and I tumbled in a mess of limbs to the ground. I snuck a look toward the trees and found Lucy staring back at me, anger wrinkling her forehead. I drew a slow breath, and then I made the decision to run.

Getting to my feet was slower than it should have been, but I managed to be faster than Christopher.

Shock wrote itself across Lucy's face as I raced toward her. My legs felt like jelly but I pushed forward. I heard Christopher swear followed by the familiar thump of his boots. *Faster.* I watched Lucy stand up and saw the flash of silver as she readied the thin blade of the sword she carried. Don't look back. I knew he was close, his footfall sounded like he was within reach of me. If I looked back, I knew that he'd have me. The leaves of the trees were almost within reach, I could just make out each scar on Lucy's face.

"Weapon!" Luke's voice echoed through the forest, ripping through the leaves. The thumping of Christopher's boots slowed and then stopped but I kept running.

Finally, I burst through the branches, sharp broken wood slicing at my skin, ripping open bits of the burned gash, and tearing more of the stitches open. Blood raced down my face and neck as I slammed full force into Lucy. We tumbled down together and the sobs came now. Long body-shaking cries consumed me. I knew I must look ridiculous but I didn't care.

I was home.

I was safe.

"We have to go, Soph. We can't stay here. We have to get Jax and Mason and go." My head snapped up at the sound of their names. They were okay. There was a look of urgency on her face, something that I didn't see often. My lungs burned as I sucked air down, trying to calm myself. Lucy pushed me off of her and got to her feet, looking around quietly before she reached down and grabbed my arm, tugging me until I was standing. "We don't have a lot of time, Sophia. We have to go now."

"Where are they? How did you find me? What's going on? Why do we have to hurry?"

She was annoyed now, I could see it in the way her shoulders tensed, the way the muscles in her jaw tightened. "Later, Sophia." More questions buzzed around in my head but I kept them to myself, simply nodding and following along behind Lucy as she hiked back into the trees.

The forest was eerily quiet, the only sound I was able to pick up was that of our boots stamping into the wet earth. One of them had to be nearby. "Lucy," I whispered.

"I know." She was almost dismissive of me, waving her hand to quiet me as she hurried along, weaving quickly around trees. I followed, the adrenaline shielding me from the pain of my injuries. Finally, we reached a small building that looked like it had once been a greenhouse. The roof was broken, shards of glass protruding awkwardly where the other pieces had fallen in.

"Six. Seven. Eight." Mason's deep voice floated on the breeze as we got closer. "Nine. Ten. Ready or not, here I come!"

Jax's giggles made me smile and I stopped to watch their game. Jax poked her head around the corner of the building, peering inside and laughing again. A wide smile spread across her face and she tucked herself back on the other side. She looked toward us and froze, her eyes widening.

"Sophia!" she screamed, stepping fully into view. She started to speed walk before breaking out into a run and smashing into me. I wrapped my arms around her tightly and squeezed, holding back the sobs that were threatening to come again.

"We were so worried about you. We thought they got you. We thought that you were dead." She was shaking, her voice tight.

"Hey," I said, leaning back and looking into her face, "I'm alright. Just a little banged up."

Horror painted itself across her face as she registered the burned cut on my face and the bite mark with the popped stitches with bruises that were no doubt encircling it, "What happened to you?"

"It was nothing," I soothed. "Just a misunderstanding with some other people. It doesn't even hurt anymore." She didn't believe me. Her wide eyes narrowed slightly and her lips created a thin line, but she simply nodded and turned back to the greenhouse.

Mason came out of the building, Jax's bag dangling from one of his hands, his own slung haphazardly over his shoulder. "We've got to get going, girls. It's only a matter of time until they find us."

"Until who finds us?" I looked over at Lucy.

"There's a huge group of shredders not too far from here. We passed them while we were looking for you. It's probably the group that was closing in at the other camp."

I nodded and ran a hand through my hair. My fingers got caught in a tangle and I huffed, wincing. My scalp would no doubt be sore for weeks. Jax took her bag from Mason and we set out, walking past the greenhouse and hopefully far away from Christopher, Luke, and the horde of shredders.

The sun beat down relentlessly on us and sweat beaded on my forehead. Muggy summer air wrapped around us, still without even the whisper of a breeze. The trees were silent, as though the whole world had frozen. The salt from my skin stung the burn on my face and I winced as each drop slipped into the wound. I'd have a scar to match Lucy now, a story to tell one day about how I fought back and eventually got away… a story that would be mostly a lie. *You resigned yourself to death… you are no great hero… you are no Lucy.*

"Did you hear that?" Mason's voice was startling and I jumped before looking at him.

"Shh," Lucy pressed a single finger to her lips and we all listened hard. The forest was not as silent as we had once believed. Leaves crunched under the weight of something large, and leaves rustled as something pushed them aside.

"The blood," Jax whispered, her eyes wide as she looked over at me, "They can smell the blood."

I cautiously touched my face and felt the warmth of my sweat. When I looked at my fingers, they were a deep red. "Shit." It hadn't been my sweat running down my face, it had been my blood. They were hunting us.

They were hunting *me*.

18

"What do we do?" Jax's voice was panicked, all the color leaving her face as she stared into the trees around us.

"We've got to stop the bleeding," Lucy mumbled, slipping one arm out and reaching into her bag. The book of matches only had one left and she looked at me sympathetically, "Come here, Soph." I made my way over to her, bracing myself for the sting of the flame. I closed my eyes, gritting my teeth. The blood sizzled as the flame touched it, evaporating as the wound was resealed. Tears dammed behind my lashes and I forced myself to stay still. "That should do it, but I have to do the one on your neck too." I nodded, squeezing my eyes shut even tighter. "I'm sorry." I couldn't hold back the scream this time.

"Lucy!" Jax screeched. "You're hurting her! Stop!"

"Jax!" Lucy snapped. "Enough!"

I could hear Jax's sobs. "It's alright Jax," I soothed. "I'm alright. It just stings a little bit." There was a few seconds of silence before she sniffled. I took a steadying breath, counting to ten, before I opened my eyes, willing the tears not to fall. *You've cried enough for today.*

Lucy tossed the empty matchbook back in her bag and adjusted the straps. "We've got to keep moving. Hopefully, they'll smell... something else."

Hopefully, they would smell *someone* else and they would go after them instead of us. *What is wrong with you?* I had devolved into a creature that actively hoped for the demise of others, actively wished that the monsters would take someone, *anyone* but me. At my very core, I was more interested in my own preservation, I would gladly let others die for me without too much of a fight when it came down to it. *You already did.*

"Come on." Mason took off ahead of us, and we trailed behind quietly, straining to hear if we were still being followed.

We walked until my feet hurt and my legs felt like jelly.

"Can we take a break?" Jax asked, her steps dragging.

"You'll have to just suck it up a little longer," Lucy sighed, swiping the sweat from her forehead with the back of her hand. The humid summer air was suffocating and I looked up at the sky, hoping for rain.

"Look at this!" Mason called from a few feet ahead. We drudged over to him and he pulled the curtain of trees to the side, revealing the remains of a camp.

"How old do you think it is?" I asked, stepping closer.

"Old," Mason replied. Dried blood coated the side of the tent, splattered across it in a horrifying wave. Pieces of clothing caught in the long-dried mud stood like proud beacons, alerting the world of what had happened here.

"What happened?" Jax asked, gripping my hand tightly in hers. I squeezed it softly, trying to comfort her.

"Something bad," Lucy said, turning away. "We have to keep moving."

"Wait," Mason said, jogging over to the tent.

"Mason," Lucy huffed, crossing her arms and shifting her weight to tap her foot. He flashed her a bright smile before vanishing inside the tent for a minute, popping back out with a sleeping bag in hand. *Why must he do this every time you find a camp?*

He laid the sleeping bag on the ground, smoothing the bright blue fabric out before rolling it up and tying it closed with the flimsy pieces of nylon hanging from it. He stuffed it into his backpack alongside the four or five others he had collected.

"Why do you have to have so many sleeping bags?" Lucy asked.

Mason glanced at her and smiled as he threw his bag back on his shoulders. "Just in case."

She rolled her eyes and spun away from him, muttering something under her breath as she tromped back through the trees away from the camp. Mason

18

grinned at Jax as he hurried to catch up and fell into his usual lumbering pace.

We walked until sunset, and the pastel sky went black. The crickets came to life and I let myself relax a little. Mason offered me one of his extra sleeping bags and I happily took it. *Maybe stopping a thousand times to look for sleeping bags wasn't such a waste of time.* I melted into the warm cocoon as my eyes grew heavy. *Safe.* These were the people that had come looking for me, that had never truly given up hope that I was alive.

"I'll take the whole watch," Lucy said, kneeling beside me.

"No." I reached a hand out to her, touching her shoulder. "Let me help you. You don't have to do it all by yourself."

"You look like shit, Soph. You need to sleep. Your dark circles have dark circles." She smirked at me. "Besides, I like looking at the stars." I could tell she was lying but I was too weak to fight her so I smiled and nodded.

"How did you find me?" I asked drowsily.

"I saw them take you from the school, I was coming to tell you about the message I saw on one of the walls. There's a safe place, a town. We have to get there."

"Eden," I murmured, struggling to keep my eyes open, "Rachel told me to find it." I didn't hear her response as my exhaustion won the battle.

Sleep came easily, dragging me into the darkness of my mind. His face dwelled there, his cold brown eyes boring into me. I could almost feel his hands in my hair, his fingers tightening around my throat. Luke lived there too, his pale blue eyes mocking me as he watched… begging to keep me as some kind of living trophy of their conquest. My skin burned where they touched, the nerves committing the feeling of them to memory, tattooing their cruelty into me forever.

My eyes snapped open, searching wildly through the darkness for them. I expected to see their faces among the shadows. My chest heaved under the weight of my fear, my throat closing as I gasped desperately for air. I clawed at my skin, willing the pain to bring forth a cry, a whimper, anything to shock me back into reality. *No matter how hard you scrub, the filth they left behind will never be washed away.*

"Soph?" I heard her, but the edges of my vision had grown blurry as panic raced through my system. "Soph, are you alright?" My blood rushed in my ears, pounding into my head. "Sophia!" I felt her hands on my skin, holding my hands to stop me from ripping my skin apart. "Sophia, look at me!" She pulled me to a sitting position and looked into my face. "Sophia, breathe!" My heart hammered against my ribs like a caged bird and I feared it may explode. "Sophia!" She was yelling now, shaking me.

Finally, air filled my lungs and relief flooded me. I sucked in one desperate breath after another, staring into Lucy's face as tears poured down my own. Long drawn-out sobs shook my body. No matter how hard I tried, I couldn't make them stop. My mind raced, desperate to banish the image of their faces back into the darkness it had created for them.

"What's going on?" It was Mason's voice, his words heavy with sleep.

"I don't know, I think she was having a nightmare. Just go back to sleep."

"Are you sure?"

"Yeah," Lucy said. "I got it." I heard Mason flop back onto the ground as he snuggled back into his sleeping bag. Lucy fixed her hard gaze on me, "What happened to you? And don't you dare lie to me Sophia because I'll know."

I bowed my head, too ashamed to look at her, knowing that if I stared into her eyes too long, everything would come spilling out like the water behind a broken dam. "It was nothing. I don't really want to talk about it, Lucy."

"Obviously it was something, Soph. I thought you were dying. I thought something was wrong."

"It'll be fine. I just need a little bit of time and everything will be fine. It was just a really bad nightmare." *You sound like Mara.*

"Look at me." It was a command and I drew a deep breath before looking back into her face. Her gaze bore into me, searching for the truth that she had to know I was hiding from her. "Tell me the truth, Sophia."

"That is the truth." I steeled myself as she stared at me, unblinking, her forehead wrinkling as my lie settled in the air between us.

Finally, she sighed, "Alright, I'll let it go this time. But next time, you *will* tell me." I nodded and she let me go. I felt unstable, like pieces of me would come tumbling down if the slightest breeze blew. She slunk away, glancing back at me only once before returning to her chosen lookout spot. I settled myself back into the sleeping bag. Sleep tried to claim me again but I kept it at bay, too afraid to let my mind slip back into the darkness, terrified to face them again.

The hours felt like days as I lay there unmoving, listening to the sounds of the night. Crickets sang all around us and pine needles shifted softly under the feet of the world's nocturnal creatures. Somewhere close by, a louder sound came. A branch snapped loudly beneath the weight of something heavy. I jolted up, staring at Lucy as she crept towards the sound, her hand poised to pull her blade.

Everything was still for a few breaths. The sound of the crickets stopped and the hair on my arms stood on end. Lucy stumbled backward, whirling to face me. "Run!" More branches snapped and I scrambled out of the sleeping bag, shoving my feet into my boots and rushing to shake Jax awake. "Jax get up!" Lucy yelled as she ran towards us.

I shook her until her eyes opened and she stared at me in shock. "Run Jax," I said urgently. She nodded and flung her sleeping bag open, bolting out of it. Together we ran blindly. The trees flew past us and I scanned the darkness for somewhere to hide, anywhere to hide.

"My whale," Jax whispered urgently. "We have to go back for my whale."

"We'll come back for it later."

"Help!" The voice was unfamiliar. I grabbed Jax's arm and dragged her along with me. "Help!" The unsettling sound planted fear in me and I held Jax tighter.

"Sophia, we have to go back and get my whale," Jax pleaded.

"No!" I barked. "We will get it after the horde is gone."

Jax tugged her arm, trying to free herself from my grasp and I held on tighter. The roar of footsteps was all around us, branches snapping, leaves being torn from trees, and snagging on skin and clothing. There was nowhere to go. Our only hope was to outrun them.

"You better run faster little girl!" a voice sang loudly. I jumped, it sounded so close. I scanned the dark trees, desperate for somewhere to stash Jax. *You can lead them away if you don't have Jax.*

"Look! Up ahead!" Lucy called from right behind us. I strained to see what she did and a pond came into view, its water glistening in the moonlight. I veered towards it and dragged Jax in, pulling her until our feet no longer touched the bottom. Something splashed in after us, and I could only assume that it was Lucy and Mason.

I looked at Jax, putting one hand on either side of her face and making her look into my eyes. "When I say so, you have to hold your breath. You can't come back up for air until we know it's safe. They won't come into the water, there's nothing in the water they want." She nodded. "One..." She drew a deep breath. "Two..." She squeezed her eyes shut. "Three..." I pulled her down with me, sinking into the depths of the water, allowing its icy fingers to pull us down into salvation. The others followed, and we stayed, suspended in the dark, waiting for the horde to pass. Jax began to twitch. *She's panicking.* I held her tight, refusing to allow her to surface. It hadn't been enough time. They'd be too close, they'd hear her and come back up for air.

She thrashed violently in my grip, fighting for her life. I held her as tight as I could, smashing her smaller frame into mine and hoping she wouldn't drown before we could surface.

19

Panic made me gasp, bubbles exploding past my lips as Jax thrashed against me with everything she had. *If you don't get her back to the surface she'll die.* I managed to hold her until she went still. *You're going to let Jax die for you?* I wrapped one arm around Jax tightly and used the other to aid in pulling us through the heavy water toward the surface. After what felt like forever, my head broke the surface.

There was silence.

I towed Jax towards the shore, kicking with everything I had in me to get her there. The muscles in my arms and legs were screaming as I tried to keep our heads above the water.

Splashing sounded behind me followed by Lucy's voice. "What happened?!"

Tears were streaming down my face, mixing with pond water. "I need help! Lucy, I need help!" I sobbed. "It's Jax!"

"I'm coming, Soph!" I could hear her splashing through the water. When she reached us, she slipped an arm around Jax's limp form and began to help me pull her to shore. *You have to go faster.* Some relief hit me when my feet touched the sand at the bottom and I was able to put more effort into pulling Jax. *She isn't breathing.* We dragged her onto the beach and flopped her there. Her skin was waxy and pale, the blood drained from it by the icy water.

"What do we do?" I sobbed, my frantic mind going blank on how to save her. Without a word Lucy shoved me out of the way and knelt beside Jax, slamming her hands on her chest. Lucy pressed down with one forceful pump after another. *You learned CPR.* In the moonlight, I could just make out the glimmer of tears on Lucy's cheeks. I fell to my knees and crawled up beside Jax's face, pushing her sopping-wet hair out of her eyes and staring down at her. A lump formed in my throat and I began to shake. Jax jerked and coughed. *She's alive!* A strangled sob burst from my lips as relief washed through my system. Water spilled from her mouth as she rolled to her side. She heaved and wretched, curling in on herself as she expelled the water. Lucy threw herself on top of Jax, wrapping her arms around her tighter than I'd ever seen her hold anything. Her face was red, the tear stains streaking down her cheeks and disappearing at her chin.

Her whole frame shook as she held tightly to Jax. " I thought we lost you." The pain that crept into her voice stabbed my heart, and I crawled closer to them, laying down against Lucy's back and just existing beside her. They were all safe. *Mason!* My head snapped up and I scanned the water for Mason, searching for him in the darkness. The only sound I could hear was Jax's ragged breathing and I sat upright, twisting at the waist to search for Mason.

Lucy examined me. "What's wrong?"

"Where's Mason? Did he come out of the water with you?"

She sat up, eyes searching just as mine had, scanning the shadows between the trees and the still water. "I don't remember if he surfaced with me."

You have to find him. The thought to yell his name flitted through my adrenaline-fogged mind but I pushed it away. *Yelling will draw too much attention.* I got to my feet and walked toward the water.

The surface was like glass, reflecting the almost starless sky back at me. "Mason?" I whisper-yelled. "Mason, where are you?"

Silence was my answer.

I glanced back at Lucy as she helped Jax sit up, silently begging her for answers on what I should do. She frowned and scanned the trees to the left and right of us before looking back at me. I paced to the treeline and peered into the shadows, holding my breath as I listened for sounds of life. "Mason?" I spun around to face Lucy again. "Where could he have gone?"

"I don't know Soph."

"You don't think he drowned do you?" Jax croaked out. Her voice was a hoarse whisper, and I refused to look into her face, knowing that I would find fear and tears there.

"I don't know," I admitted, scanning the water's surface again. "He did go into the water, right Lucy?"

"I think so."

"What do you mean you think so? He was with you wasn't he?"

"Yes, he was with me, but I'm not a damn babysitter. We were all running. I hit the water first, I thought he was right behind me." I fought to remember the moments leading up to pulling Jax under with me. Trying to think through the cloud of panic that had engulfed me, trying to remember if I had ever seen Mason come into the water. There was only Jax there, her face filling up the entirety of the memory, the fear in her eyes engulfing me so completely that she was all that I saw... all that I heard.

"What if he never made it to the water?" I whispered. The words were shaky, uncertain. My heart began to pound, thumping in my ears.

"What do you mean? Where else would he have gone?" Jax's voice was rising in pitch, the ends of her words crackling. She looked around, pulling out of Lucy's grasp and trying to stand up.

Lucy pulled her back into the sand and put her finger on her lips. "We still don't know where the horde is."

"What if they got Mason?" She was almost yelling now.

Lucy slapped her hand over her mouth and made her look at her. "Shut up Jax. Letting those things know that we are here is not going to help find Mason. Do you understand me?" Jax nodded and Lucy slowly removed her hand, eyeing her suspiciously as she did. "We are going to get up and very slowly walk in a direction. You have to stay with us."

"Okay," Jax whispered, bowing her head. Lucy got to her feet and reached down to help Jax up. Jax refused the help and struggled to her feet on her own. Without even looking at Lucy I knew she was scowling, agitated that Jax was acting like a belligerent teenager. I spun in a slow circle, trying to decide on a direction to start looking for Mason.

"Just pick one," Lucy snipped. I flinched and scurried off in the direction that I was facing. I heard Jax and Lucy follow me, their shoes dragging through the sand, my own being swallowed as I waded through. The night was still too quiet, the usual sounds silenced by the predators stalking through the trees. We vanished into those same trees, hoping that we wouldn't have to venture too far inside. I was hyper-aware of every step that I took, careful to avoid large branches and piles of leaves. I knew that silence wouldn't save us in the end—they would find us by smell—but some small part of me still clung to the hope that if we were quiet enough they wouldn't bother looking for us. My heart sank when I heard a twig snap right in front of me. I froze and took a shaking step back, bumping into Jax and sending her pinwheeling into Lucy. Another snap sounded through the dark, this one somehow much closer than before.

"Run," I pleaded with Lucy. "Take Jax and run."

"What about you?" Jax demanded wrapping her hands around my wrist and holding on with everything she had.

"I'll be alright, I'm just going to lead it in a different direction. I'll meet you back at the pond okay?" I knew it was a lie as I was saying it and I looked at Lucy, hoping she could read the desperation in my face. She slung one arm around Jax's middle and used the other to slap her hand over her mouth and cut off the wail that we both knew was coming. She heaved Jax along behind her as she headed back the way we had come. I turned away, staring back into the darkness just ahead. The hairs on my arms stood at attention and every muscle in my body screamed at me to run, begging me to save myself. This time I stood still, steeling myself against what I knew was coming for me.

Save Jax.

Save Lucy.

Save your family.

When it slammed into me, I wasn't ready. The force of its emaciated frame was something that I had not been expecting. I tumbled back, skidding through the carpet of broken twigs and dry needles. The smell of rotting flesh filled my nose and I fought the urge to gag. I threw my hands out in front of me just as it lurched for me, pushing me flat on my back. The skin that touched mine was gnarled and covered in large, open wounds that leaked a nauseatingly dark liquid. Its teeth smashed together in a sickening click, warm, blood-tinted drool dripping onto my face. I turned my head back and

19

forth, trying to keep the drool from touching the cuts on my face and neck. *The last thing you want is to be one of them.*

"You smell so good," it hissed at me in a voice that sounded not quite human. It struggled above me, laughing as though it was having fun. It reached toward my outstretched arms and I panicked, allowing it to fall face-first onto me. I rolled and tried to get to my feet. I felt its hand wrap around my ankle yanking me back down into the leaves.

"Let go!" I kicked at it, grinning when I felt my boot make contact. It didn't cry out in pain, it only kept coming as I crawled on my belly, trying to get back up as I went. Tears stung my eyes when it grabbed me again, dragging me back. I searched the pine needles and dead leaves for some kind of weapon. All I found were sticks. *This will have to do.* I wrapped my hand tightly around the largest stick that I could find and rolled, flipping onto my back so I could look it in the face when it died. It lunged at me, mouth open to reveal two rows of broken, jagged-edged teeth.

I made myself watch as I swung, forcing the blunt end of the stick deep into its left eye socket. It opened its mouth in a wide 'o', its eyes going wide for just a split second before it collapsed. Its head landed on my thighs as it fell, and I scuttled away, letting it fall limply onto the ground. I sat in silence, waiting for my breathing to return to normal, listening for the sounds of others.

20

My heartbeat slowly returned to normal, and I breathed a sigh of relief, the pain fading from my chest. The sound of leaves crunching under something heavy tore through the still night air and I bit the inside of my cheek to keep from screaming. *Why does this always happen to you?*

I fumbled blindly through the underbrush looking for something to protect myself for a second time and found a decent-sized rock. It was smooth and heavy in my hands. I crouched behind the thick trunk of a tree and prayed that whatever was coming would ignore me this time. The energy I needed to keep myself alive was fading, the claws of my demons reaching out to grab me. *You saved yourself, so why didn't you even try to save them?* I tried to push the thoughts away but they kept coming, slamming themselves into me. *Selfish.* Fear began to wrap me in its familiar embrace. *Coward.* Breathing became harder and I shook my head, trying to bring myself back from the brink.

"Sophia?" I snapped to attention at the familiar voice, the fog clearing from my brain. "Are you okay? What happened?"

"Mason!" The tears came, large drops rolling down my cheeks as the rock fell from my hands.

His hands were warm and I shivered despite the heat of the night. "What happened? Where's Jax?"

Jax! "With Lucy." He nodded and hugged me, nestling me against his chest and wrapping his arms around me. He smelled like damp earth, sweat, and something almost metallic; his t-shirt was soaked at the collar. "Where did you go?"

He lifted one arm and rubbed the back of his neck, looking away from me. "I led them away from you." He peered back down at me and offered a small smile, flashing his teeth and letting his hand drop back down. "They were so close, I didn't think we'd all make it into the water before they saw us so I ran in a different direction." He bit his bottom lip and shook his head. "I lost them and you were gone when I circled back to get you." His attention suddenly snapped to me, his eyes going wide. "Why?"

"Jax," I took a ragged breath, "she almost," I could barely bring myself to finish the sentence, "died."

"How?!" He gripped my arms and held me out away from him. His eyes roamed my face. Sweat beaded on his forehead, and his jaw clenched. His eyes grew wider as he stared at me, and I squirmed uncomfortably.

"Because of me." If Lucy hadn't been there, Jax would have been dead. *You would have killed her too.*

Mason pulled me back against him. "She's alright now though. She's alright Sophia." I nodded, though I didn't feel any better. I couldn't be trusted to look after any of them. I couldn't risk a repeat of what happened on the beach. They were too important to me. "Where did Lucy take her?"

"Back to the beach. I heard a shredder and told them to go back. I—I didn't want Jax to see me die." *But you didn't die.*

"We should go find them. Those things are still everywhere. It's only a matter of time until one of them catches our scent." He released me from his warm embrace and stood up, offering me his hand. I took it and hoisted myself up, steadying myself before letting him go. Mason smiled at me and set off in what I assume was the direction of the pond. I was all turned around from the fight and probably would have wandered aimlessly looking for the others if he hadn't come along. I followed a few paces behind him, hoping Lucy and Jax had made it to the pond. Worry ebbed at the edges of my mind, testing the walls for a way to slip in. *What if they were attacked?* "Did Lucy tell you about the writing at the school? About the town?" he asked suddenly.

I shook my head to clear it. "Yes."

"Do you think that it's real?"

"Yes." *Anything could be real at this point.*

"Soph!" It was Lucy's voice. She sounded relieved and I peered around Mason. She and Jax were huddled near the water's edge. "You found Mason."

"Actually, he found me," I murmured, hurrying to them and throwing my arms around both of them. I squeezed with every bit of strength that I could muster. I had never felt such relief and happiness. It lit up my brain like the midday sun, banishing the shadows back into the abyss they had crawled out of. This time when the tears fell, they were filled with joy. Lucy shifted, trying to move away from me and I released them, mumbling an apology as I plopped down on the wet sand beside Jax.

"Where were you, Mason?" Lucy demanded, standing and brushing the sand from the backs of her legs.

"Protecting you," he spat, squaring his shoulders.

She glared at him. "You could have told one of us the plan. We thought you were dead."

"I didn't think there was time. Next time I'll make sure to hold a meeting before I do something." He glared at her, and she glared right back.

"You don't have to be an ass about it. We had to go looking for you and I thought Sophia was dead because of it." Lucy growled.

I could hear the rage creeping into her voice, the harsh tone edging toward cruel.

"You don't have to be stupid Lucy. I did what I thought I had to do to keep you alive." His fingers curled into fists at his side and he blew out a hard breath.

Lucy practically bristled as she stalked toward him. "What did you say to me?" She stopped inches from him, her head tilting back to stare up into his face. She didn't give him a chance to answer before her hand made contact with his cheek.

He winced but made no other movements. "Feel better?"

I stared at him through the darkness and sucked in a sharp breath through my teeth when I spotted the tear in his jeans, the blood shimmering in the light when he shifted.

21

"Lucy, get away from him!" I lurched toward her. She looked back at me, tilting her head to the side, her tongue pushing the side of her cheek out slightly. "Lucy! Get back! That isn't Mason!" She looked down at his leg and it finally seemed to click in her brain. She tried to run but Mason's large hand snagged her by the throat and lifted her until her toes were the only thing touching the sand.

"Mason, no!" Jax's voice broke as she screamed at him. *Make it all go away.* Jax tried to run at him but I threw my arm out and knocked her to the ground. "That isn't him anymore. You can't go near him." I grabbed her and pulled her back to me, panting as I dragged her slowly through the sand.

"He's going to kill Lucy!" she cried, large tears rolling down her cheeks and dripping from her jaw.

I grabbed her chin, making her look at me. "Stay here." I got into a crouching position and then looked back at her. "Close your eyes." I saw the argument forming on her lips. "Close your eyes, Jax." She nodded and shut her eyes, covering them with her hands. She looked so much like a child that it broke my heart. *She deserves better.* She was afraid more than she was happy, and we were dragging her through this hell with only our hope that it would get better eventually. *Selfish.* I ran to Lucy and tried to pry Mason's fingers loose. They were slick with sweat and I couldn't get a good grip. "Mason let go!" He laughed at me and squeezed harder, Lucy's face was starting to turn a light shade of blue as she thrashed and kicked in his grasp. "Mason!" I screamed, not caring if the entire world heard me anymore. "Mason let her go!" He was stronger than I thought he would be, his knuckles turning white as he squeezed. I let him go and started searching Lucy, my fingers probing for the metal of a blade. Her sword wasn't strapped to her back like usual. I looked around for something else and found nothing. Lucy's movements were getting slower. *Shit, shit, shit, shit.* I kicked his bloody leg and he loosened his grip. Lucy stopped moving and Mason dropped her, letting her crumple to the sand.

He set his sights on me and smirked. "You've always gotten on my nerves Sophia. I can't wait to rip you apart." I stumbled away from him, still scanning the sand for some kind of weapon. He advanced on me, a predator after his prey. I stumbled in the sand, my shoes getting caught and dragged down into it. He began to circle me, making me turn with him to keep him in my sight. "I can't wait to see what Jax tastes like." A laugh bellowed out of him and he flashed a toothy smirk. "I wish I could make you watch me bathe in her blood." He closed in on me, creeping closer with each passing second.

"Jax run!" I screamed, praying that she would get away while he was busy with me. *She'll die without you and Lucy to protect her.* His face was too close to mine, his breath caressing my skin. *She'll die if she stays here. At least out there she has a chance.* The scent of rotting flesh and blood drifted around me and my stomach turned. He walked his fingers down my arm slowly, the promise of death written in the way he dragged his nails softly on my skin. *You are going to die. You are finally going to pay for what you did.* I took a step back and he mimicked me. Before I knew what was happening he was on top of me, slamming me down into the sand, his weight pressing me painfully into it.

"I think I'll start," he dragged a single finger down the length of the scab on my face, "here." When he pulled his hand away my blood glistened on his skin. He smiled broadly at me and his tongue flicked out to lick it clean. He closed his eyes and groaned, "You taste like Heaven, Soph." *He sounds like Luke.* The name slammed into me, knocking the air from my lungs. Bile rose in my throat and I almost choked on it. Chills raced up my spine and I turned my face away from him. He laughed, a deep throaty sound and I felt his tongue touch my uninjured cheek, slowly traveling from my jaw up to my forehead. Christopher's face flashed in my mind, his dark eyes amused at my torment. Memories of the way his hands touched my body mixed with

21

the horror of Mason's touch, drowning me in a new wave of terror.

"Just get it over with!"

"But where is the fun in that Sophia?" He leaned close to my ear. "Maybe I just want to play with you a little longer." I closed my eyes and more images of Christopher and Luke flashed behind my lids. Mason's face found a place among theirs, settling into its new home. *You won't have to suffer much longer.* Death would at least silence the demons lurking in my mind. *Hopefully, he kills you fast.* The thought of dying a slow death made tears dam behind my lashes. *What if he makes you one of them?* That thought made the breath hitch in my throat until it felt like I was going to suffocate.

I couldn't fathom wandering the earth hunting down innocent people to murder, torturing and toying with them just to feast on their blood. The only consolation that I had was that Jax would hopefully have enough time to get far enough away that she stood a chance. Lucy was still laying in the sand, her lashes fluttered against her cheeks. If I stalled him long enough, she might have time to wake up and run. *Then Jax won't be alone.* I shimmied in his grasp, trying to get my knees between us to push him off. He only laughed and snaked a hand around my throat, pushing until my breath was coming out in little wheezing puffs.

"You are going to beg for death, Sophia."

I squeezed my eyes shut as he snapped his teeth right beside my ear, the click making me wince.

Something hot dripped on my face but I was too afraid to open my eyes, too afraid to see my demise coming right at me. Mason went limp on top of me, his head smashing painfully into mine. I yelped and my eyes shot open. Everything was fuzzy, his face too close to mine to see any detail. I wiggled under his weight.

Mason didn't move.

"I—I'm sorry!" Jax was sobbing. *Sorry about what?*

22

My mind raced a million miles a minute as I tried to piece the events together. I blinked a few times, staring at the blob of color floating in my field of vision. *What is that?* After what felt like an eternity, my senses returned and I shoved Mason off of me, letting his limp form roll into the sand. I sat up and slapped my palms together, brushing the sand off and smearing blood all over. *Is that your blood... or his?* I bit the inside bottom of my lip and closed my eyes, taking a deep breath. I steeled myself and turned my head, peeking at Mason.

Scarlet poured out around the point of a screwdriver, seeping into the sand. I wretched, my stomach convulsing as I threw my head forward and dry heaved. When the bout of nausea had passed, I dragged my arm down my face, wiping the blood away before it had the chance to reach the cut on the other cheek. I focused on Jax now, her wide eyes brimmed with tears. Her nose scrunched up, contorting her face with such fierce agony that her lips visibly trembled as she staggered backward.

"It wasn't him, Jax," I whispered, getting to my feet. I held my arms out in front of me, palms facing her and took a small step closer. She shuffled away from me and covered her mouth with her hands. She sucked in two rasping breaths, one right after the other, and tears poured down her face. "Jax, it's okay." I soothed, taking another step.

"No, it's not!" she wailed. She fell to her knees before slumping forward, pulling her arms in tightly and wrapping them around herself. She shook with the force of her sobs, gasping for air as she trembled. Her fingers gripped her upper arms, digging in. I dropped down to my knees in front of her. When I touched her, she jerked away from me, but I pushed forward. Her whole body quivered when I hugged her, wrapping my arms around her and holding her tightly to me. She lifted her head and turned her face into my shoulder, her tears soaking the fabric.

I began to rock back and forth slowly, shushing her as I did. I knew the pain she was suffering, the guilt that was beginning to eat her alive. The thoughts would come at her like an ocean, the memories a storm, sending hundred-foot waves crashing over her head, pulling her down into the depths. *She will suffer.*

"I'm so sorry Jax."

"He was going to kill you. I couldn't let him kill you!" Her selflessness would be her downfall, I could feel it in my bones. *But for today, she is your savior.*

"But I am so happy that you didn't listen to me this time." I knew that I should have been mad at her for not running, for risking her own life for mine, but I couldn't find the energy to be angry.

"Soph? Jax?" I turned and found Lucy sitting up, her hand rubbing the sand from her face as she glanced around. Her eyes widened when she saw Mason's lifeless body. "What happened?"

"He was one of them. He must have gotten bit or scratched. I didn't notice it when he found me. I should have noticed it." I replayed the moments after Mason had found me, searching the fear-hazed memory for some sign of the injury. There was nothing. *This is your fault. You should have seen it. You brought him back to the others.*

"He was going to kill everyone," Jax stammered, lifting her head to look at Lucy.

Lucy's eyes softened as she looked at Jax. "You saved us." Her tone was gentle, as though she was trying to coax a wounded animal out of hiding. "You were so brave."

"Can we bury him?" Part of me knew the question was coming.

Lucy tilted her head, biting at her lip. I knew she was thinking about whether or not we would be able to. "Of course, we can." It was my voice that said the words, my voice that promised something I wasn't sure we would be able to do. Jax smiled at me and my heart shattered; darkness sat in the depths of her once sunshine eyes. "Why don't you find a spot to bury him? I have to check on Lucy." She nodded and climbed to her feet, wandering off almost dreamily in the direction of the pond.

When I made my way over to Lucy, she was scowling. "Are you insane? How the hell are we supposed to bury him? Why did you tell her yes?"

"What was I supposed to do Lucy? She just killed someone she loved. She wanted a funeral for a rabbit she never met. Did you really think we'd be able to talk her out of something for Mason?" I stared at her, willing her to understand, to remember who she was talking about.

She dropped her head a bit, her eyes softening, the line of her jaw relaxing. "Honestly," she took a breath, "no. But we have to be quick about it." She slowly made her way to her feet, ignoring me when I reached out to try and help her steady herself. "We don't have all night. More of those things are probably close by."

When I looked for Jax, she was standing at the water's edge, staring out at the glass surface.

I stood beside her, "Have you decided on a spot?"

"Yes," she turned to me. "Here."

"In the water?"

"You and Lucy suck at whispering." She managed a half-hearted smile for only a second before it slipped. "I know we don't have a lot of time. But he still deserves something."

Staring at her I found my heart breaking more than I ever thought possible; standing beside me was not the sweet little girl Lucy and I had found lost in a crumbling apartment building, but someone damaged and threatening to come apart at the seams. "I am so sorry Jax."

"It isn't your fault Soph."

She didn't say the words, but I knew she blamed herself, "It isn't yours either." *She had no choice.*

"I know." She turned away from the water and walked back toward Mason. I trailed her with my eyes, watching her fall to her knees beside him and lean down to rest her head against his shoulder. I heard the low murmur of her voice as she whispered something, but I couldn't make out the words.

22

Perhaps it was only a goodbye or an apology for what had happened to him. Lucy walked over to her and laid a hand on her back, rubbing in small circles.

She looked over to me, "Come on Soph, we've got to move him." She looked back at Jax. "Where are we taking him?"

"To the water." Lucy stiffened and studied Jax for a moment. She slowly nodded while casting me a sideways glance. I shrugged as I walked over, crouching down and wrapping my hands around his ankles. Lucy grabbed his wrists and we lifted him. He was heavier than I had expected him to be and it took everything that I had to get him over to the water's edge.

"Do we just walk him in as deep as we can and drop him?" I asked.

"I guess," Lucy answered, stepping into the water. Jax trailed us closely, tears slipping silently down her cheeks. She was shaking again. This night would be burned into her memory for the rest of her life. Slowly, we walked until the water was well past our waists. "Say goodbye, Jax. We can't go much deeper."

"I already said goodbye."

Lucy nodded at Jax and released Mason's wrists. I took a deep breath and let go of his ankles.

After a moment, his large frame slipped below the surface, vanishing into the inky depths. "Goodbye Mason," I whispered into the darkness.

23

"We should leave," Lucy murmured, wading through the water back to shore. Jax walked closely behind her. I lingered a moment longer, staring down into the depths of the pond. In the darkness, I couldn't see Mason, but I knew he was there, not far below the surface. *He didn't deserve this.* I touched the water's surface with my fingertips, watching it ripple out away from me. *If only I'd found you sooner.*

"Soph! Hurry up!" I turned to look at Jax as she called for me from the sand. Her hands were on her hips, her head cocked to the side.

"I'm so sorry Mason." A few tears dripped from my chin before I turned away. The warm, humid air was a stark contrast to the icy chill of the water that had caused my legs to go numb.

"Where did you find the screwdriver?" Lucy asked, glancing at Jax.

Jax frowned. "It was laying on the ground next to Mason before we left camp. I grabbed it just in case. I didn't want to use it." She folded her hands together, fidgeting with her fingers.

I walked up beside her and placed my hand on her shoulder. "It's alright Jax. You did what you had to." *That won't make the pain any easier to bear.*

The silence was almost suffocating and I was grateful when Lucy's voice broke it. "Let's go. We'll circle back to our camp, grab what we can, and look for a new spot." Jax shrugged off my hand and I let it drop limply back to my side. Lucy vanished into the trees, heading back in the direction we originally ran from. *Hopefully she knows the way back.* I hadn't paid enough attention when we were running to remember anything except the leaves smacking against my skin and the fear eating me alive. Chills raced through my whole body and I wrapped my arms around myself as we walked, gripping my upper arms for comfort.

"Look," Jax breathed, stopping short in front of me.

"What?" I yelped, almost slamming into her back.

She pointed toward a cluster of bushes and I squinted my eyes to see what she was talking about. Suddenly, a little flash of light burst to life and Jax sucked in a breath beside me. "What is that?"

"Haven't you ever seen a lightning bug before?" Lucy asked, standing beside her.

Jax shook her head and took a tentative step forward. "Do they bite?"

Lucy laughed softly. *She hardly ever laughs.* "No. I used to catch them when I was a little girl." She walked closer to the bush as more lightning bugs lit up. "Here, I'll show you." She cupped her hands and scooped at the air, collecting a few of the bugs. She turned back to us and held her hands out to Jax who crept closer. I drew nearer, smiling as Jax positioned her head over Lucy's hands. Light erupted from Lucy's palms as the insects flew off and Jax laughed, throwing her head back and grinning widely.

"I want to try," she announced, turning her attention to the bush. She tiptoed closer and grabbed at the air, pouting when she missed.

Lucy smirked. "Try again."

Jax nodded and made a second attempt, squealing with delight when she closed her hand around one of the flickering lights. "What did you do with them?" she asked, cradling her hand close to her chest.

"I took a jar outside with me and caught as many as I could to put inside it. Then I made a wish and let them all go."

"A wish?" Jax questioned bouncing on the balls of her feet.

Lucy nodded.

"What kind of wish?" Jax asked, looking down at her hand.

"Anything you want," Lucy whispered.

Jax's eyes grew wide and she looked at Lucy seriously. "Promise?"

Lucy nodded again, before holding her hand out, offering Jax her pinky. "Pinky promise."

Jax squealed again and hooked Lucy's finger with her own, shaking once before focusing her attention back on the treasure in her hands. She closed her eyes and whispered something too soft for us to hear and then uncurled her fingers. The little bug flashed its light and then took off and rejoined the others. *Family.*

"What did you wish for?" I asked.

Jax grinned. "I can't tell you. If you tell a wish, then it won't come true." *She's still so innocent.*

"We should get going," Lucy said, turning her back on the bush and starting to walk again. Jax didn't move for a second, the blinking lights reflecting in her eyes as she stared at the bush. When she finally blinked, a small smile touched her lips and she turned to walk along behind Lucy. I gave the fireflies one last glance. *Jax can still be happy.*

By the time we made it back to the clearing, the sun was already peeking over the horizon, the sky lit up in cotton candy colors. Everything lay untouched in the grass, the sleeping bags thrown about from the chaos of our departure. Lucy grabbed Mason's bag, paused for a moment to stare at it, then flung it over her shoulder along with her own. I knelt beside my sleeping bag and rolled it up, shoving it back into my bag and slipping it on. When I glanced over at Jax, I caught her sitting where Mason had slept, her head bowed, fingers white-knuckling the fabric of his faded forest green blanket. She wiped her face with the back of her arm and shoved the blanket into her backpack, zipping it shut and throwing it onto her back. She stood up and walked over to Lucy, mumbling something to her. Lucy only nodded and then looked over at me and offered a sad smile. I wanted to tell her that I was sorry, that if I had been more observant she never would have had to do what she did.

Your fault.

Lucy hurried toward me, Jax close at her heels. "I think we should go to Eden."

I nodded. "Do you remember the directions on the message? Mason said there were directions, I—" I snapped my mouth shut when Jax jerked at the mention of his name. I wished that I could take it back.

"I remember most of them. I'm sure once we get closer, there will be more messages."

"Should we go back to the school?"

Lucy shook her head. "No, I've been leading us in the direction of Eden. I should have told you once you got back, but I figured you'd want to go anyway."

"Hopefully it's still standing," I mumbled.

Loneliness weaseled its way into my thoughts as we started walking. As we went, I tried to fight the images of the night from my mind but couldn't. *Was that the last thing that your parents saw? Were they afraid like you were?* The thick fog of the past seeped into my consciousness and I was powerless to stop it.

Coward. Coward. Coward. The word pounded into my head with each heartbeat, hammering into my brain until it consumed me. *Monster. Monster. Monster.* I felt the world falling away, piece by piece, the towering trees slowly replaced by dull wood grain. The smell of blood filled my nose and I thought I'd choke on it. Clothes brushed my face as I watched my hands slam the door shut, sacrificing them for myself. I stood for a moment, only the space of a heartbeat, trying to make myself open the door, willing myself to die with them… but I couldn't. I couldn't make my muscles respond, self-preservation held me captive as I imagined the horrors that awaited me on the other side of the door.

I heard items crash to the floor, the sound of heavy objects hitting the hardwood making me jump. *What kind of person sacrifices their loved ones just to save themselves?* I was a monster. Almost inhuman growls resonated from the other side of the door and the floorboards creaked under the weight of the invaders.

24

Thunder clapped overhead and my heart jumped with it. I looked up. Clouds engulfed the sky, swallowing it in shades of gray. The air was heavy with the scent of rain. Lightning burned across the gunmetal sky, cracking like a whip as it went.

"Should we find somewhere to hide?" Jax asked, gazing skyward.

Lucy shook her head. "It's just a little rain. We aren't going to melt."

Jax frowned. "My mom said it wasn't safe to be outside when there's lightning. You could get struck."

"You aren't going to get struck by lightning," I offered, walking up to her.

"But my mom said," Jax argued.

"Look," I said, pointing to a tree. "See how tall that tree is?" She nodded. "See how tall you are?" I put my hand on the top of her head for emphasis. She nodded again. "Lightning strikes the tallest thing. All these trees are taller than us so the lightning will strike them."

Her eyes widened. "Won't that cause a fire?"

I chuckled. "It could."

She fidgeted with her fingers, picking at her nails before mumbling, "I think we should find somewhere to wait."

"No," Lucy said sternly. "We can't stop every time there's a storm." Jax's bottom lip jutted out and she looked at me with pleading eyes. I shrugged and looked at Lucy. "No," she repeated. "This isn't the first time there's been a thunderstorm. You'll be fine."

The sky opened up, raindrops pouring down on us. I smiled and turned my face up, letting the water wash over me. *Maybe it will wash away the*

24

memories. Thunder growled again and I laughed, looking at Jax. Her hair hung in two dripping curtains on either side of her face, droplets running down her cheeks and falling from the end of her nose.

"What's so funny?!" she called over the torrent of rain.

"You!" I laughed. Jax beamed, flashing her teeth. I looked at Lucy.

She pushed her hair off her forehead and grinned. "At least we'll be clean when we get to Eden!"

The rain came down harder, making it hard to see. The drops slammed into my skin and I jerked at the sting. "How long do you think this'll last?" I yelled.

"I don't know!" Lucy called back. "Follow me!"

I nodded and grabbed Jax as I moved, pulling her with me. Lucy stopped at the base of a large pine tree, the thick branches offering some shelter from the storm.

"I thought we weren't stopping," Jax teased.

"I fibbed," Lucy said with a sigh.

Jax laughed and leaned out to look up at the sky. "How much longer do you think it's going to be?"

"Hopefully not too long," I mused.

Another bolt of lightning sliced across the clouds and Jax jumped, stumbling back. Thunder rolled and she took a step closer to Lucy, biting the inside of her cheek. "It better not be," she grumbled. There was silence for a few minutes before Jax spoke again. "Soph?"

"Hmm?"

"What do you think happens when you die?"

I jerked my attention to her. "What?"

"Do you go to Heaven?" She pinched her eyebrows together, taking a deep breath. "Is that where Mason went?" She stared at me, a few tears slipping down her cheeks.

Tears welled up in my eyes and I blinked a few times, trying to get rid of them. "Mason went somewhere beautiful," I whispered.

"Do you think my parents are there too?" She looked down at her hands as she fiddled with her fingers, intertwining them again and again.

I tried to swallow the lump in my throat, my chest growing tight. I opened my mouth to answer, but it was Lucy that found the words first. "Of course they are," she soothed, pulling Jax into a hug. She squeezed her and rested her chin on top of her head, humming the tune to a song I didn't recognize. They stood like that for a long time, swaying back and forth to Lucy's song. *It's your fault Jax had to kill him.*

After a while, the rain began to let up and Lucy released Jax, poking her head out from the cover of the pine tree. "I think it's safe to start walking again."

I mumbled my agreement and stepped out into the light mist. Fog crept along the ground, swirling around our ankles when we stepped in it. Jax laughed and jumped, creating a cloud that wrapped around her like a soft white blanket. Lucy shook her head, smiling to herself and started off into the trees behind Jax. *They'd be better off without you.* I hesitated. *You only bring them pain.* My heart sank.

"Sophia!" Lucy called. I looked up. Her head tilted to the side as she stared at me, arching a brow. "You're going to get lost again if you don't hurry up."

I pushed my tongue into the back of my teeth before nodding and hurrying to catch up to them. The rain made the air even thicker with humidity, and I kept wiping my face to get rid of the water droplets. Jax darted off ahead, weaving through the trees.

"Don't go too far ahead!" Lucy yelled after her.

"I won't!" She ducked into a thicker area of trees, her giggles floating out of the tightly woven branches.

Then everything went silent.

"Jax?" Lucy yelled. There was no answer. "Jax!" She picked up her pace and I followed. "Jax!" We slammed into the trees, pushing the branches away from our faces as we clawed our way through.

"What do you think happened here?" Jax asked as we burst through the final wall of trees. She looked back at us.

I shook my head, clearing it as my eyes focused on the scene in front of me. "I'm not really sure." I scanned the ruins of the camp. "It looks like it was ransacked," I answered. Clothes, blankets, dishes, and other items littered

24

the grass while the open tent doors blew in the faint breeze.

"No," Lucy said suddenly. I looked at her questioningly and she sighed, "Look." She bent down and picked up a book of matches, holding them up to show me. "You don't ransack a camp and leave things like matches behind."

"Was it shredders?" Jax questioned, stepping closer to us.

"No," I said. "There isn't any blood."

"So why is there so much stuff?" she asked.

"Someone wanted people to think this place was empty," Lucy mumbled, dropping the matches. Jackets, rope, silverware, and other useful equipment lay scattered in the dirt, each one carefully placed to sell the charade. Now that I was really looking at it, I couldn't believe that I had fallen for it.

"It's a smart idea I guess," Jax began, venturing closer to the tents. "Do you think it really works?"

"I'm not sure, we'd have to find them and ask," Lucy answered.

"If they're even friendly," I snorted.

"They have children," Jax said, suddenly popping her head around a tent.

"How do you know?" I asked, moving toward her.

"Because of this," Jax announced, holding up a small dress. The fabric was worn and stained in spots with mud and who knows what else. The garment couldn't have belonged to a child older than eight. The little puffed sleeves were torn in places but the bulk of the pale blue fabric remained intact.

"We should leave them be," I said, looking around more cautiously. "If they have children they might be more dangerous than we thought."

"But the horde!" Jax cried. "What if they don't know about it? We can't just let them be massacred." I looked at her and huffed. *She's made up her mind.* Her lips were drawn in a hard thin line, her eyebrows pulled down to shade soft brown eyes that burned into my very soul. Her forehead pinched as she stared at me, daring me to fight her on the subject.

"They probably won't come back if they know we're here Jax," Lucy huffed.

"Well, we have to find some way to warn them. I'm not just going to let them all die." The corners of her eyes crinkled as she glared at Lucy.

"What do you propose we do then?" Her tone was harsh, but the twitch in the corner of her lips told me she was going to give in to Jax's demands. *She always gives in to Jax.*

25

We settled in for the time being, hiding from the heat of the day in the shade of the trees. It felt like summer would never be over, the humidity hanging thickly in the air and wrapping around us like a hot wet blanket. The sun had reached the mid-point in the sky by the time I heard the low murmur of voices and the crunching of leaves underfoot. From my vantage point in the bushes, I was the first to see them return.

The first one into the clearing reminded me of a deer, each step cautious, as though monsters would jump out at her at any moment. *Smart.* She fully entered my field of vision, though the bulk of her face was obscured by the moss-green hood she had pulled tightly around her. Strands of thick hair spilled from the shadow of the hood, some a fiery auburn, others a glistening snow white. I could see the next one slightly better, she was probably close to my age with a sun-speckled face and a mop of messy brown hair piled on her head.

Slowly, the two of them began to clean the camp, chatting amongst themselves as they went. The murmur of their voices was like water over smooth stones. They gathered handfuls of the strewn supplies and set them inside the doors of the tents. The hooded girl threw her head and laughed at something the other girl said, the sound like bells. The hood fell back slightly from her face, exposing the source of the white strands. A thick chunk of hair by her face glittered a brilliant white in the sunlight. She dropped the things in her hands, reaching up to adjust the hood back to where it had been. After a few minutes, she called out with a sharp whistle. The tune sounded oddly familiar, calling forth hazy daydreams from my childhood, but I couldn't quite place the song nor the voice that had once sung it to me.

The bulk of the group flooded into the camp, each person slowly beginning to clean the mess they had left behind. I counted six of them in total. The hum of their combined voices was comforting in a way that even the night sounds were not. Their voices carried the promise of civilization… of belonging. The night sounds only carried the promise of other life.

They worked quickly, going through the motions like they had done them a thousand times before. After a few minutes, two final figures appeared at the far tree line. The older of the two moved swiftly, though slow enough for the child to easily keep up. *There's the owner of the dress.* From this distance, I couldn't see much more than the pink bow sitting atop the child's head. Judging solely by size, I wouldn't guess she was older than seven or eight.

"They're all women and girls," Lucy whispered, a bit of awe in her voice.

"How have they stayed alive so long with such a big group?" I could hear the excitement in Jax's voice as she peered around me.

"By not taking risks," I answered. "Do you remember the deer that we saw Jax?" I saw the nod of her head out of the corner of my eye. "Do you remember how slow it walked, how it kept looking around and moving its ears?"

"Yeah."

"Well, they're like that deer. They're looking for danger all the time."

"What about her?" Jax questioned, her hand zipping past my face to point at the girl that had been the first into the clearing. "She has a weapon."

I nodded, eying the crossbow flung across her back. "Afraid doesn't equal defenseless. Even deer are dangerous."

"How should we introduce ourselves?" Jax asked, her breath tickling my ear as she pressed her face closer to mine.

"You and Soph should go," Lucy offered. "That way they don't get spooked." I shot Lucy a dirty look. *You're terrible with people.*

"Ready Sophia?" Jax asked. She jumped back away from me and when I looked at her, she was shifting impatiently, practically vibrating.

"As I'll ever be," I mumbled. Lucy gave me an encouraging smile, the right side of her lips turning up while the left remained still, held tightly in place by a long white scar. Slowly, Jax and I climbed through the thick fence of bushes and headed into the clearing. *They're going to kill you.* I hoped with everything in me that we didn't look like too much of a threat.

"Who the fuck are you?!" The girl with the hood seemed to almost materialize out of thin air in front of us, her lips twisted into a snarl that made her upturned nose scrunch up. *There it is.* Her eyes were bright blue, almost electric in color and from this distance, I could make out the small white scars dotting her sunburned face.

"We just want to help you," Jax cooed, holding her hands up to show she wasn't a threat. Out of all of us, she looked the least like a danger. I mimicked her, hoping that this would be over quickly.

"Help us with what?" the girl barked. I sized her up, realizing for the first time how small she was. The sweatshirt was swallowing her, making her look like a child playing dress-up with their parent's clothes.

"There's a horde coming," Jax offered, letting her arms drop a bit. The girl jumped at the movement, reaching into the pocket of the sweatshirt and pulling a knife. She flicked it open and waved it in our direction. "Jeez," Jax chirped, raising her arms back up and taking a step back.

"Don't move," the stranger demanded, waving the knife again, a silent warning.

"Look you little psycho," I hissed. "We didn't have to hang around and warn you. In fact, I didn't want to, but she," I jerked my chin in Jax's direction, "insisted. So take the warning, pack your shit, count your fucking blessings, and we'll be on our way." *You should play nice.*

"What's going on over here Hope?" a voice asked. The second girl from the clearing came over to investigate, regarding us like someone would an animal in a zoo. *Hope. Not exactly a fitting name for the crazy girl holding you hostage.*

"These two said they saw a horde." She spoke to the newcomer but never took her eyes off of us. I wasn't even sure she was blinking.

"A horde?" the second girl asked, raising an eyebrow at us.

"Of monsters," Jax blurted out.

The new girl clicked her tongue before speaking. "Where?"

"We didn't just see them," Jax explained, "we lost one of our group to them." The words came fast, like vomit that she couldn't control.

"Okay," the new girl began, huffing, "but that still doesn't tell me where."

"We lost them sometime last night. In this area," I snipped. "They are still around so I suggest you drag your asses before they find you."

"How do we know you're telling the truth?" Hope bit out.

"Don't believe us," I shrugged, "it's your funeral."

26

The second girl sighed deeply. "Hope, please stop." She returned her attention to Jax and me, putting her hands on her hips. "The horde, how many of those things were in it?"

"I don't know," I admitted.

"Then how do you know it was a horde?" Her southern accent dripped heavily from the words and she blew a hair out of her face.

Agitation was beginning to cloud my mind. "Because we could hear them. Have *you*," I pointed at her chest, "ever even seen one of them?"

Her eyebrows shot up, "Of *course* we have." She rolled her eyes. "But we've only ever seen one or two of 'em at a time. They don't travel together."

"Maybe they didn't, but they evidently do now," I said, blowing out an irritated breath.

"We don't have a reason to lie to you," Jax blurted out.

"Sure you do," Hope growled, focusing her attention on Jax. "You probably want our camp… our supplies."

"We don't need it," Jax said matter of factly. "We're going to Eden."

Hope scoffed, "Eden? That stupid little town that has messages all over?" The other girl snickered. "It probably doesn't even exist." She paused. "And if it ever did… it doesn't now."

I could see Jax shrinking away from Hope's words, doubt twisting her features. She looked at me for help, and I sidestepped until she was shielded from the stranger's views, bracing myself between them like a wall.

"I told you not to move." She stalked closer to me, holding the knife in my direction in a silent threat. *Move again and she'll kill you.*

"Leave her alone." I hissed. "She's a child."

"Let's all simmer down here a little," the unnamed girl offered, raising her hands in a show of peace. *Why did Lucy send you to do this? You're gonna get yourself killed.*

"Then tell your attack dog to stop threatening a little girl," I hissed, clenching my back teeth together.

"I'm not that little," Jax grumbled behind me. I shot her a warning look over my shoulder and she glared at me, but was silent.

"Hope, put the knife away. If these people wanted to hurt us, that knife wouldn't do anything. Especially since there are more of them."

I jumped a little at her words. "How do you know that?" I tried to sound nonchalant, hoping she was only bluffing. *Don't look at Lucy.*

She laughed, a full sound that bounced off the land. "Because I saw all of you in the bushes when we got back. You aren't great at hiding." *She's bluffing. They wouldn't have come back if they saw you.*

"Then you should know that if we wanted your supplies or your camp, we would be able to take it. The little one wanted to help you. Take the warning and get out of here before it's too late." I dropped my arms and turned, nudging Jax to do the same. She huffed at me but headed back toward Lucy, grumbling incoherently as we went. *It's almost over.*

Before we could reach the trees' safety, Lucy came rushing out. Her eyes were wide, her blade clutched tightly in her hands and dripping with thick, oily blood. I froze, fear sinking into the pit of my stomach. *Not again.* Time seemed to slow down, my vision sharpening everything into painful clarity. The sun's rays were almost blinding, burning me until my eyes watered. My body felt heavy, each movement like I was forcing my way through quicksand. *Move!* I shook my head, trying to force the hallucination to break.

"Run!" Lucy's voice sounded so far away, echoing in my head. I couldn't make my limbs respond as she ran towards me. I watched her get closer and closer, until her weight slammed into me, sending me pinwheeling backward, my arms flying out to the side to try to save myself from hitting the ground. I finally regained control of my muscles and clumsily ran behind her. Confusion flashed across the faces of the group as we sprinted towards them but horror soon replaced it as the horde spilled out of the trees behind us.

The sound of snapping branches and feet slamming into the earth screamed their warning to run faster. My face was soaked with tears and sweat. I looked as I ran, scanning the crowd for Jax. *Find her.* The group of survivors panicked, some ran with absolutely nothing, disappearing quickly into the trees while others remained, grabbing at things on the ground.

The two that confronted Jax and I sprinted into the main part of the camp, throwing tent doors open and yelling for people to run. In the chaos, it was hard to tell one face apart from another. With each passing second my heart seemed to pound harder, slamming into my ribs until I thought they would shatter. *Jax!* She settled into my view and I veered toward her, reaching out a hand to grab her. When my fingers finally touched the rough material of her sleeve I squeezed with everything I had, holding onto her tightly.

I dragged Jax in Lucy's direction. "Where do we run?!" I called. Lucy didn't answer, but when she glanced back at me, there was fear in her gaze. She opened her mouth and then closed it again. *There is nowhere to run.* There were trees as far as the eye could see, stretching out in front of us like a wall.

"With us!" Hope yelled, appearing from a tent with the littlest of the group and the older one that had emerged with her. We veered towards them as Hope scooped up the child and began running.

"Where are we going?!" Jax yelled.

"An underground bunker near here! It's the meet-up point for the group in case we get separated!" We slammed into the treeline, and I held on tighter to Jax. We weaved through the trees faster than I had thought possible, the adrenaline flooding my system and driving me to run faster.

Keep Jax safe.

27

I bit back a scream as the leaves were torn from the trees just behind us, branches snapping as they poured into the forest behind us.

"How much further?!" Lucy yelled, looking behind us. When she looked forward again, the color had drained from her face and I had to fight the urge to look at the horror behind us.

I glanced over at Jax just as she began to turn her head. "Jax no!" Her terrified eyes snapped to me.

I'll protect you. I'll save you.

"Not much further! It should be just over here!" Hope called.

The glitter of metal in the sunlight caught my eye and we all ran toward it. Hope yanked the door open and rushed us all inside. It slammed shut with a finalness that I wasn't prepared for. Silence echoed through the space as Hope went around slowly turning small lanterns on.

Jax plopped down on the floor and didn't give anyone time to breathe before she panted out introductions. "I'm Jax, and this is Lucy and Sophia, but we call her Soph or Sophie. What about you guys?"

Forever the social butterfly. If it were up to her we'd save everyone that we had ever come across. You'd have a group of hundreds if you let Jax be in charge.

They looked at us suspiciously before Hope finally spoke. "I'm Hope, and this is Claire." The second girl we met raised her hand awkwardly as she sat down. Hope continued, "Freya." The child's protector nodded her head. "And the little one is Anna-Beth."

Jax smiled at the child, focusing all of her attention on her. "That's a beautiful name. How old are you?" She scooched closer to the girl. In the dim light, I saw a bit of life return to Jax's face. *Love at first sight.* The light seemed to flicker back on in her eyes for a brief moment as she stared at the little girl.

"Six!" Anna-Beth squealed happily, flashing a bright gap-toothed smile. Her face was smudged with dirt and one of her wide green eyes was rimmed with purple and blue.

"What happened to her eye?" I asked, glancing at Freya.

Freya studied me, her eyes narrowing slightly and her head jerking back a little. Finally, she answered. "Nothing that will ever happen again." Her voice was flat, emotionless. The air in the room felt heavy, pressing down on me as Freya stared, unblinking.

"So," it was Lucy's voice, "how long have you guys been in that spot?" I glanced at Lucy and found her shifting in her seat, tapping her fingers against her thigh.

I turned to look at the others. Hope pulled her hood off, revealing the entirety of her face. "Claire and I were the first people. We found that spot not long after those things started spreading. Then as time went on, more and more people came. Some stayed, others were just passing through on their way deeper into the forest." I was close enough to study her this time. The scars that dotted her face were abundant and small, the largest one couldn't have been more than an inch.

"Why do you destroy your camp?" Jax asked curiously.

Hope's face fell and she bit at her bottom lip. "There was an incident. We helped the wrong people."

"We thought they were some of those monsters by the time they were done. I still think they might be," Claire added. Hope snapped her attention to Claire, scowling at her, and Claire gave a sheepish smile.

"What do you mean?" Lucy asked, straightening her back, though she began to pick at the skin around her nails. I fidgeted in my seat, suddenly very uncomfortable. Something inside of me was screaming that something was very, *very* wrong. I absently lifted my finger to my face, tracing the length of the scab on my cheek.

"They were... sadistic. That's the only way I can describe it," Hope sounded far away like she was drifting into her mind, "They tormented me until they got bored and moved on. And I was lucky enough to get *these*," she gestured to her face, "to remember them by." She turned so the light shone on every inch of her skin. I squinted as I studied the scars. My gaze settled on a large one on her jaw, the skin indented in a tell-tale pattern. *Yours will look like that too.* She almost instinctively reached to run her fingers across the puckered skin. *He bit her.*

Everything came slamming down. The air sucked the life from my lungs and I choked out the name, "Luke."

Hope went still and turned to look at me. "Christopher."

"What did they do to you?" I asked softly.

"Things that I only remember in my nightmares." Storm clouds gathered in her gaze, the electric blue irises slipping into darkness.

"Is that why you freaked out in your sleep Sophia?" Lucy demanded, glaring at me. "You were attacked? You were *hurt?*"

I nodded, my fingers reaching to touch the rough scab on my neck. "They're monsters. Poison. But they're gone now. The forest is too big for them to be able to find me or Hope again."

"I hope you're right," Hope murmured, getting up to pace. The wild dual-colored waves of her hair were tied loosely into a braid, bits of it falling into her eyes and she pushed it back with a shaking hand. She resembled a pixie, a small, delicate face with dainty features that reminded me vaguely of drawings in my fairy tale books as a child. It wasn't hard to see why Christopher and Luke had picked her to torment. They were large and dominating compared to me, but they would have consumed Hope.

"How did they find you?" Claire asked, looking at me curiously.

"It was an accident," I sighed. "I was trying to warn Lucy about them but she had already gotten out. I couldn't fight them off. I tried but they were stronger than I was."

"How did you get away then? Did they let you go?" Hope stared at me now, millions of questions written on her face.

"No," I said, shaking my head. "They belong to a camp with other people. There was a girl there, Mara, she helped me get out. She saved me."

27

"A girl? Did they hurt her too?" Lucy questioned, leaning forward, resting her elbows on her knees, and settling her chin in her upturned palms. She tapped her fingers rapidly against her cheeks, sweat beading on her forehead.

"Yes," I started. "They did something to her, but she wouldn't tell me what." *You know what they did. They did it to you.*

Hope stopped pacing. "Were there other people in the group?"

"Yes, two others besides Mara. Rachel and Michael. Did they mention anything about a group when they were here?"

"No," Claire said matter-of-factly.

"Yes," Hope whispered. "They told me that they were going to bring me to meet girls like me. I thought they were just trying to scare me, I didn't think they actually had a group of people. Did they hurt the other girl too? How bad was Mara hurt?"

I nodded, frowning at the memory of Mara's empty gaze. "Mara wasn't really there anymore. And Rachel," I paused, "Rachel suffered a lot because of them."

"How many other people do you think they tortured?" Lucy asked.

"I don't know," I mumbled. The part of my brain that Christopher and Luke dwelled in had wondered about their other victims, but the thought was too painful and I had locked it away with them. *Those two probably have a list of victims to rival that of a shredder.*

28

"That thing you said before," Hope said, glancing at Jax, "about Eden. Are you really going?" She took a step forward, craning her neck.

"Of course we are. Lucy said we were." Jax smiled broadly at Lucy, showing all of her teeth. "She'd never lie." *Her hero. But what are you?*

Hope turned her attention to Lucy and me. "So you think it's still there?"

Lucy shifted uncomfortably in her seat, straightening her back and crossing her legs. "I don't know," Lucy finally sighed.

"Then why are you going?" Freya asked softly, brushing a curl out of Anna-Beth's sleepy eyes.

"Because it's a chance," Lucy explained, taking a deep breath. "A chance for something better for the people that I love." *She loves you.* The weight of that simple phrase settled onto my shoulders. *Lucy loves you.* The memory of every reckless thing I had done flashed in my mind, each one chipping away at me. *Would Lucy have been hurt if Christopher had killed you? What about if Luke kept you?* I had been moving through this life thinking that I had nothing to lose, that I already lost everything with any meaning. I stupidly believed that the people I laid down my life to protect would never do the same for me. All of the nights that Lucy stayed up and kept watch slammed into me. *She didn't think you were too weak.* I stared at Lucy quietly, watching the way she glanced at Jax every few moments, biting her lip until it was raw. Her gaze settled on me for a fraction of a second, only a heartbeat, and there was something confusing in the way she stared at me. Something halfway between worry and pride.

"You should come with us." Jax's voice was like bells and both Lucy and I snapped our attention to her.

Hope shifted her weight from foot to foot, almost bouncing. "I don't know about that." *Smart girl. Cautious girl. Why couldn't you be more like her?*

"Jax, we don't really know them and they don't know us." Lucy's voice was tight, though it was laced with honey as she spoke to Jax.

"You didn't really know me when you found me either. But you still took care of me," Jax argued, crossing her arms. "And you didn't know Mason either," she said softly, almost whispering.

"You were a child," Lucy snapped. "A little girl. These are grown adults." Jax flinched away from Lucy, wincing at her tone.

"Anna-Beth isn't," Jax whispered.

Lucy huffed and looked at me, her gaze singeing me with its intensity. "What do you think, Sophia?"

"I—I," I stuttered, "I don't think we should really be talking about whether we are taking people with us in front of them."

"It's alright," Claire snorted. "It's not like there's anywhere else to talk." When I glanced over at her, she had a smirk on her full lips. "But if you want my opinion, I'd take us with you."

"And why is that?" Lucy challenged.

"Because there are only three—" she tilted her head, "well, two and a half," she chuckled, smiling at Jax who stuck her tongue out in return, making Claire laugh harder, "of you and Eden is at least a two-week walk from here. You've got to go through a lot of populated areas to get there." A little bubble of fear rose in my chest. *Population equals shredders.* I rubbed my forearms and tried to shake the anxiety away. *Everything will be alright.*

"Then why would we want more people to have to watch and keep safe? That's more chances of getting killed or found by the shredders."

"Shredders?" Claire asked, raising a brow. "Is that what you call 'em?"

"What do you call them?" Lucy bit back.

"Hey, calm down. I didn't mean anything bad by it." Claire raised her hands in mock surrender, grinning ear to ear when Lucy rolled her eyes. "We don't have a name for them."

"I don't think the group will agree to go to Eden," Hope offered.

"Then they don't have to," Claire shrugged, letting her hands drop back down. "But we have to at least give them the option."

"I didn't say you could come with us," Lucy snapped.

"Who said we were going with you, Princess?" Claire chirped, winking at Lucy. I stifled a giggle as Lucy's face went bright red and she looked at the floor.

"We can't just leave people behind," Hope growled, seemingly unaware of the comedy show going on.

Claire threw her gaze back to Hope, a wide grin still plastered on her face. "We wouldn't be leaving them, Hope. They would be choosing not to come with us. We knew that we wouldn't be able to stay here forever."

"We are not going to abandon them," Hope insisted.

"Hope," Claire said sternly, "you cannot protect everyone. Sometimes you've just gotta let people do what they wanna do. And if they don't wanna come with us, then you can't make them."

Hope threw her hands up, letting them slap back down on her thighs and sighed, "How are we going to tell them?"

"God Hope, why is everything such a process with you? Ya just tell 'em." I watched Hope struggle, her mouth opening and shutting again a few times before she finally gave up and turned her back to us. "Ignore her, she's a little dramatic sometimes." *You don't say?* Claire fixed her gaze back on Lucy. "So, what about you coming with us?"

Lucy scoffed, "We already had this conversation."

"No," Claire laughed, "we talked about us going with you. Now we are going and you're invited to come with us."

Lucy's eyebrows shot up as she stared at Claire, "What?"

"You heard me, Princess," Claire drawled in her thick southern accent. "You're invited to come with us."

"Why would we want to do that?" Lucy snorted.

"Because there is safety in numbers," Claire said, clapping her hands together.

"No," Lucy sighed, "there is death in numbers."

"I think they should come with us," I offered.

28

Lucy whipped her head to look at me, "What?"

"I think Claire is right, there is safety in numbers. There will be more people to find food, no one would have to go alone. More people to keep watch so it isn't always you."

"I knew I liked you," Claire chuckled, throwing me a glittering smile. "So it's settled then," she said, tossing her head and laughing. "Y'all are coming with us."

"That isn't what she said." Lucy's tone had gone sour.

"No need to pout, pretty girl," Claire cooed. "We'll go with you if that makes ya feel better." Lucy stared at her in silence for an uncomfortable amount of time before grumbling under her breath and crossing her arms. *She's throwing a temper tantrum.* I covered my mouth with my arm and tried to stifle the laughter. Lucy rolled her eyes and refused to look at me. Across the room Hope pressed her back to the wall and slowly slid to the floor, leaning her head back and closing her eyes.

29

It felt like a small eternity had passed when Anna-Beth's babydoll voice rang out through the silent room. "When can we go back outside?"

Freya gently patted the child's hair, shushing her.

Hope rolled her eyes and pushed herself off of the floor before wandering over to the door. After a brief pause she slowly opened it, poking her head out to look around. "I think it's safe."

Lucy and I both stood at the same time and walked over to her, trying to peer around her. The sun was just beginning to sink below the treeline, rays of golden glow reaching out for us. The oblong shadows of the trees raced across the ground, running from the coming darkness.

I strained to hear the sounds of the forest and breathed a sigh of relief when I heard the chirps of crickets and the distant call of a bird. "It's safe," I whispered.

Before Hope had the chance to say anything, Lucy was shoving past her. "Jax, come on!"

I watched curiously as Lucy stood among the trees, sucking down air like she had been starved of it.

I followed her out, creeping close to her to whisper, "Are you alright?"

She threw me an exasperated look. "I'm fine. I was just sick of being locked in that tiny space with everyone. I needed fresh air."

"Are you sure?" I knew that the question was heavy. *No one could be fine after the last two days.* I pressed anyway.

"Yes." Her tone shifted, growing more irritated. If I kept pushing I knew she would explode, I was walking through a minefield. I decided to drop it and turned to walk back to the bunker. Jax emerged next, Anna-Beth hurrying along behind her. *I'm sure Freya will enjoy her break.*

"See if there's anything left worth salvaging in the camp!" Lucy called. I lifted my hand and waved in acknowledgment.

"Come on Jax, bring Anna-Beth if it's alright with Freya and we'll look around the camp." Jax beamed and raced to Freya. Out of the corner of my eye, I caught Freya's nod and I waved to her. "Don't worry, I'll keep an eye on her!"

"Thank you!" Freya yelled back with a small smile.

The girls raced back to me and we headed back through the trees toward the camp. The forest was in shambles with leaves and branches torn from trees and flattened into the damp soil.

"Look Anna-Beth," Jax said. I glanced back just in time to see Jax hand the smaller girl a large pine cone. Anna-Beth grinned and clutched her newfound treasure to her chest, both little hands wrapped tightly around it. *They'll be best friends.*

"Wait up!" Claire called. I paused, her and Hope jogging up to me. "We'll go with ya. I wanna see if anything is salvageable. Plus there are a few things I want for sentimental reasons."

"Alright," I said with a shrug. It wasn't a long walk back to the camp. *It felt longer when you were running for your life.*

"Oh," Hope breathed, freezing as we reached the edge of the forest.

I frowned as I stared at the ruins of the camp, the shredded tents blowing in the breeze, empty packages rolling across the grass. "You and Anna-Beth stay here," I said, glancing at Jax. "We'll be right back." Jax nodded and plopped down in the grass at the edge of the trees.

"Do you think everyone got out?" Hope asked softly.

"I hope so," I mumbled, heading toward the center of the tent circle. Broken glass crunched under my boots as I walked, scanning the ground for anything that might be useful. Hope picked a few small things up and stuck them in the pocket of her hoodie while Claire vanished into one of the half-destroyed tents. *There's not much left to save.* I managed to find a few items that hadn't been too badly destroyed. I rounded the back of one of the tents and my boot splashed into a puddle of something. I frowned and looked down, my heart skipping a beat when I saw the large red splotch in the grass. As my eyes drifted across the ground toward the trees, streaks of it glittered in the sun. *Not everyone made it out.* I spun on my heel and headed back the way I'd come.

"Hope!" It was Claire's voice that ripped through the trees. I turned and saw her stumble out of the darkness, blood coating the front of her shirt. *When did she go in there?* Her eyes were wide, her blood-covered hands shaking as she held them out in front of her. I felt my feet moving before I was aware that I decided to move them. Claire stumbled further out of the trees, tears streaming down her face, little hiccuping sobs emanating from her. "Please help them."

I knew what I was going to see before I ever saw it. The smell of copper hung heavy in the air, almost thick enough to gag me. Scarlet was sprayed across the tree trunks and dripped from the tips of leaves, creating little pools in the pine needles.

"I should have been here to help them." Hope's voice was flat. *Empty.* I could see the emptiness creeping into her eyes, the hollow parts slowly beginning to consume her entirely.

"Then you would be dead too." My own voice sounded foreign to me.

"But maybe they wouldn't be." Staring at Hope, I saw myself looking back. Hope melted away, her electric blue eyes replaced by my haunted hazel ones, her two-toned curls morphing into my bone-straight blonde bob. I saw my guilt begin to swallow the girl in front of me, drowning her in the crashing waves, and pulling her down into the murky depths. I reached toward her, trying to pull her free and save her from the encroaching ocean.

"No, you'd all be dead," I whispered.

She looked at me with tears welling up in her eyes. "How do you know?" She looked so lost, so broken. *She looks like you.*

"There are no survivors of shredders."

She melted into herself, wilting like a flower starved of water. Her knees seemed to give out and she crumbled to the blood-soaked earth. When I spoke, it wasn't to Hope, it was to the broken little girl that hid in the closet

29

that day. "You can't blame yourself for what happened. You can't hold onto the pain that they endured. You would have died with them, and they never would have wanted that for you." As I stared at her, the blood-spattered trees melted away and smooth dark wood replaced them, the darkness slamming down around us.

Gurgling screams filled the air, ripping through it. As I fell into the shadows of my mind, something was different this time. I was on the outside looking in, watching myself go through the motions that cost my family their lives. The door to the closet slammed shut, my hands holding it closed before dropping to my side. I watched as I just stood there, staring blankly at the door, as though I was confused about what had happened. I wanted to scream at her to open the door, to go back out there and fight for them. *But she would die trying.* I turned from the door before sinking to the floor, pressing my back against it. I watched blood seep in from beneath the door, drenching me in crimson, yet I did not move. My heart broke as I watched myself fall to pieces, sobs shaking my body as I curled in on myself. With each heartbeat another chunk of me fell away, leaving large gaping wounds behind. I watched in horror as the little girl in front of me gave her soul away piece by bloody piece. *She was just a child.* I knelt down beside her. *She didn't deserve this.*

I reached out to the broken girl. "It isn't your fault." My voice sounded alien; out of place in the dark chaos. This version of myself continued to sob, shaking as the screams were cut off with a final wet gurgle. "They loved you. They never would have wanted you to die with them. You're just a little girl!" When I looked up to meet my own gaze, the storm clouds I had become so accustomed to in familiar hazel eyes seemed to clear a little, the burden of the choice lifted from shoulders never meant to bear it. *I was just a child...*

30

Painful bursts of light flashed in my head and distantly, I heard a familiar voice. I looked around, searching for the source. The voice came again, closer this time. *Lucy?* I shook my head, trying to clear it, but the girl with the haunted hazel eyes remained burned into my consciousness. *You.*

"Sophia?!" It was Lucy. I could hear her now as she got closer. "Sophia we have to go!" *Why?* I looked down and saw the blood coating the front of me, staining my hands. My legs were wet, my knees planted firmly in a small ocean of blood and pine needles. *How did you get down here?* I looked up again and found Lucy's face staring at me with urgency.

"What's wrong?" I asked.

"We've got to go," she looked at me and sighed. "We've got to get you changed and then we have got to go." She reached down towards me and I nodded, grabbing her hands and letting her pull me up. My legs felt like Jell-O and I wobbled as I tried to regain my balance. Lucy tugged me along, leading me out of the trees and back to the others. The fog was finally lifting from my mind and I scanned the group. Jax stood beside Freya, clutching Anna-Beth tightly in her arms. Hope and Claire were huddled together nearby, their eyes still shining with tears. The blood had been cleaned from Claire's skin and when she noticed me, she gave me a sad smile.

"Where are we going?" I asked, shaking my head again to clear the rest of the haze.

"Anywhere but here. We can't risk them coming back to look for more food." Lucy dropped my hand and picked up a pile of clothes, shoving them into my arms. "Now put this on." I nodded and started stripping down, peeling the blood-drenched clothes from my skin and replacing them with the new ones.

"Here, this will help," Claire's soothing southern twang echoed in my ears. She held a large plastic bucket out to me.

I peered inside and smiled gratefully at the water. "Can you help me?"

She nodded. "Sure thing hun."

I tilted my head forward and waited. The cooling kiss of the water washed over me and I reached to scrub at my scalp, rinsing the blood from the golden strands. I cupped my hands and rinsed my face and rubbed water up my arms, scrubbing at the skin until it was red and sore. *You have to get rid of all of it.* After the water ran out, I stayed where I was for a few seconds, breathing deeply.

"Let's go. We don't want to be here too long," Lucy urged. I threw my head back, slicking my hair back from my face and looking around. Hope was flitting around, grabbing things and throwing them into the backpack she was dragging along with her. Jax and Anna-Beth sat quietly in the center of the destroyed camp, drawing in the dirt. I searched for Lucy and found her watching the chaos of the group.

"Where's Freya?" Claire asked, looking around.

Hope popped her attention to her before looking around as well, "She was just right here."

"She's gone," Jax whispered, almost too soft for me to hear.

"Where did she go Jax?" I asked taking a step toward her.

She looked at me and then back at Anna-Beth. "She said that she couldn't stay anymore. I don't know where she went."

I whirled around to Hope and Claire. "Where would she have gone?"

Claire sighed. "She never really wanted to be here."

"What about Anna-Beth?" I asked, looking back at the little girl curled up beside Jax.

"She's her sister. Their mom died when Anna-Beth was only a year old. She went out to get food and never came back. Freya has blamed Anna-Beth ever since." Claire offered. "She probably saw this as her opportunity to get away."

"We have to look for her!" Hope cried.

"No," Claire snapped, "she made her choice. I'm not wastin' my time trying to find someone that doesn't wanna be found."

Hope grumbled something under her breath and continued to shove things into her backpack. *Do something useful.* I looked around until I spotted a backpack and picked it up out of the dirt. After brushing it off I began packing it with random things I found that I hoped would be useful.

"Hurry up," Lucy growled, pacing back and forth between the ruins of the camp and the blood-drenched trees.

"Calm down, Princess," Claire chimed, slinging her backpack over her shoulder and flashing Lucy a thousand-watt smile.

"Don't call me that," Lucy hissed through clenched teeth.

"Alrighty then, Sunshine." Claire's lips turned upward in a sly smile as Lucy's face went bright red and she turned away from her. I hid my own grin as I finished shoving things in the bag and zipped it closed.

"Are we ready now?" Lucy demanded, crossing her arms. No one answered, we all simply walked toward her.

I stopped beside Jax as she got to her feet and she reached for Anna-Beth's hand. "Come on Anna," Jax coaxed.

"What about sissy?" Anna-Beth asked, her doe-eyes wide and wet with unshed tears. Jax looked at me, biting down on her lip hard.

I squatted in front of Anna-Beth. "She had to go away. But you are going to come with us. Okay?"

"Is Jax coming too?" she asked, wiping at her face with chubby hands.

I nodded, "Yes, Jax is coming too." The girl nodded and clung desperately to Jax's hand. Jax gave me a sad smile and started walking to where the others were waiting. *Poor little girl.*

The walk was uncomfortably quiet, the only constant sound was that of Anna-Beth chattering happily to Jax about flowers and animals that she saw at one time or another. Jax seemed all too happy to have the tiny human. When we stopped for the night, the stars were glittering across the moonless black sky.

"This will do for tonight," Lucy sighed, slipping the backpack from her

30

back and letting it flop onto the ground. "I'll take the first watch."

Before I could say anything Claire's sweet voice chimed in, "I'll help you, Sunshine."

"You don't have to," Lucy insisted, glaring at her.

"I want to," Claire said, setting her own bag down.

Lucy sized her up, scanning her from head to toe before sighing, "Fine. But don't talk to me."

Claire laughed, "I can't promise that, but I'll try my hardest."

"Let's get you two settled," I said, leading Jax and Anna-Beth to a spot. I helped Jax get unpacked, holding onto Mason's blanket tightly for a minute when I pulled it out of Jax's bag. I swore I could smell him on it. I laid it out on top of her sleeping bag.

"No Soph," Jax said, grabbing the blanket. "It goes here." I watched as she folded it into a small square and laid it at the top of the sleeping bag like a pillow.

"I'm sorry," I whispered, reaching into the bag and pulling her whale out. I set it on the blanket, hoping that's at least where it went. I set to work getting Anna-Beth's bed ready, laying out the small sleeping bag and pink blanket.

"It's okay. You didn't know," Jax said smiling.

"What's that?" Anna-Beth cooed, pointing at the whale.

Jax grinned and grabbed it, setting it in Anna-Beth's lap. "This is my whale. My dad got it for me before I was born. It's how I remember them."

Anna-Beth ran her hands over the tattered stuffed animal and smiled softly. "It's really nice. I wish I had something to remember my mom and sister."

Jax frowned. "Why don't you sleep with him tonight? Maybe he'll make you feel better. Then we can find you a special stuffed animal on our way to Eden."

Anna-Beth squealed with delight and scurried to her bed, clutching the whale tightly. She settled herself under her blankets, flipping onto her side and snuggling the whale close to her face.

31

The sun was just beginning to crest the tops of the trees when Lucy's voice ripped me from my sleep, demanding that we all get up. I sat up and groggily rubbed my eyes, before tossing Lucy a half-hearted glare. *It's too early.*

"Let them sleep a little, Sunshine. They had a rough day yesterday," Claire said with a yawn and a sleepy smile.

Lucy glowered at her and Claire lifted her hands and laughed softly before collecting her bag. The dark circles under her pretty eyes said that she had been up all night alongside Lucy. *Wonder how well that went.* I drug myself up, my back aching from the hard ground. The sleeping bag only provided so much cushion and I was pretty sure I had laid mine on a ton of rocks. I rolled my shoulders, rubbing them and trying to release some of the tension.

"We don't have forever," Lucy snapped. I whipped to look at her, ready to snap back but found her looking at Claire who was laying in a thick patch of grass with her eyes closed. "We don't know where the horde is."

"A little rest won't hurt anything," Claire said, drawing the words out lazily.

"I'm not arguing with you," Lucy sighed, throwing her hands up and rolling her eyes.

Claire smirked, opening one eye to peer at Lucy. "But I love arguing with you, pretty girl."

Lucy huffed and stalked off, eliciting a soft laugh from Claire, her eye closing again as she relaxed. I busied myself looking through my backpack and making sure there was enough room to shove the thin sleeping bag into.

"Anna-Beth and I are picking flowers," Jax announced, bounding up to me, Anna-Beth hurrying clumsily along behind her.

"Okay," I said, "but make sure you let Lucy know and don't go into the trees. You don't know what's in there."

"Will do!" Jax called racing off toward Lucy before I could finish my sentence. I watched Lucy sigh but nod her head. She hardly ever told Jax no. The two girls ran off toward the trees and eagerly began plucking flowers. *Their happiness is beautiful.* I finished packing up and wandered over to Hope.

"What do you want?" she snipped, shoving her blanket into her bag.

"How are you doing after yesterday?"

Her hands froze for a second, her fingers tightening around the fabric. She sighed and looked up at me, her bright gaze burning me with its intensity. "I'm fine. Now drop it please."

"If you ever need to talk…"

"I said drop it!" she snarled, glaring at me and shoving the last bit of the blanket into the backpack and zipping it closed. I wanted to say more. *Don't push her.* I bit my tongue and nodded, leaving her alone.

"Help!"

I jerked in the direction of the voice.

"Help!"

Hope stood up and looked around.

"Anna-Beth?" I asked curiously, looking at Lucy. She glanced at me before looking around and mouthing the numbers for a headcount. *One. Two. Three. Four.* Her eyes widened and I could see the panic spread across her face. *She was two short.* Jax and Anna-Beth were no longer picking wildflowers by the tree line. "Anna-Beth?!" I yelled walking in the direction that they had been only moments before.

"Help!" Her little voice was getting closer. I breathed a sigh of relief when I saw her burst through the trees. *Five.* I opened my arms to her, squeezing her a little when she slammed into me. Her little hands latched onto me and clawed into my skin, holding on for dear life.

"Anna-Beth?" I smoothed her hair with my hand. "Anna-Beth, what's wrong?"

She sobbed into my shoulder, her face buried in the fabric of my shirt. I stared expectantly at the trees, waiting for Jax to come out, but the leaves didn't even rustle. *Where's Jax?*

"Help me!" Jax's voice cut through the early morning fog, the sheer desperation in the words making my blood run cold. Lucy blew past me before I could really understand what was happening.

I released Anna-Beth, pointing at Claire who was now standing and starting to walk toward me. "Watch her!" I yelled, taking off after Lucy.

We both ran blindly through the trees as another scream tore through the air. My heart thundered in my chest, each beat slamming into my rib cage and echoing in my ears. Panic settled into the pit of my stomach like a snake ready to strike as yet another scream came through the trees.

"Jax!" The pain in Lucy's voice sliced into me. *Please don't let it be too late.* "Jax!" This time Lucy's scream was tinged with tears, her voice tight from the fear. My own chest was aching, adrenaline surging through my body. The screams from Jax stopped and yet something pulled me forward. I burst into the clearing seconds behind Lucy and my knees buckled. The grass was soft, the softest thing I had touched in a long time.

Time seemed to stand still as the smell of copper hit my nose. Lucy's screams sounded so far away, so guttural and painful, like a piece of her was being torn from her body. I could see her running out of the corner of my eye, her blade sweeping at the hazy silhouettes of the figures surrounding Jax. Their voices were muffled as my heart roared in my ears, they were begging, scampering back from Lucy as she held the blade like some avenging angel.

Finally, I made myself look at her, made myself look at Jax. I could barely see her through the ocean of tall grass, her tiny frame hidden amongst the hues of green and gold. The long thick waves of her hair, lit up like fire in the early morning sun, drew me in her direction. I willed myself forward, my nails digging into the wet soil as I crawled through the dew-soaked meadow, the warmth of my tears a stark contrast to the cold embrace of the tall grass.

"Jax..." Her name was barely a hoarse whisper as it fell from my lips. My palms splashed into the small puddles of blood that had collected around her. *Six.* Jax was curled in on herself, her knees pulled to her chest, arms covering her head in a desperate attempt to save herself. She was drenched in blood, strands of her hair dripping with it. "Jax please." *It's too late.* I reached a

31

shaking hand out to touch her, gently pulling her arms away from her face. A sob tore out of my chest, my throat tight as I screamed out Lucy's name. Blood was smeared across her face, speckles of it mixing with the freckles across her cheeks and forehead. Bruises were already starting to blossom across her skin, large purple and red splotches littering the exposed skin. *Her neck.* I touched the deep red circling her throat, running my fingers across the damaged skin, a sob forcing itself past my quivering lips. I looked over at Lucy, a silent prayer shared between us. She only shook her head and dropped her eyes to the ground.

I heard the scream, a primal, soul-shattering sound that took me a minute to realize was coming from me. I felt the panic begin to take hold, familiar hands reaching up from the shadows and grabbing hold, burying themselves deep inside of me. My breaths came faster and more shallow as I looked down at Jax, my entire body shaking. My chest tightened, my throat closing. *You're suffocating.* I couldn't draw a deep enough breath to keep myself alive. My eyes widened as more sobs began to force their way past my lips, tears drenching my face. Everything became painfully bright and focused, the blood-stained face of the sweet girl I loved burning itself into my memory with painful clarity. With each sob my lungs burned, screaming at me to breathe and yet I couldn't make myself.

32

I don't know how long I sat there, suffocating in the haze of my own pain. Every part of me had gone cold and numb. *Gone.* I was faintly aware of Lucy's presence in the clearing, her angry voice bouncing around me as I remained unmoving, kneeling beside the girl I had loved so desperately. All I could see was Jax. Her smiling face swam in my head, her sweet laugh wrapping me in the warmth of its' comforting embrace. Memories of Jax flooded my brain.

"Sophia!" It sounded like Lucy, her voice threatening to break the wall of memories. "Sophia, I need your help!" I shook my head almost dreamily, watching a thousand different versions of Jax dance in front of my eyes. "Sophia please!" I felt pressure on my arms and I lifted a hand to swat it away as Jax's melodic laugh bounded around my brain. "Sophia!" The pressure grew more intense, pressing into me until I yelped and the illusion was shattered, all of the images and memories of Jax crumbling and falling like shards of broken glass, each one slicing at my heart until I feared there was nothing left of it.

"Why would you do that?!" I screamed, rage bubbling in my chest. "Now she's gone!" I whirled on Lucy, shoving at her arms. *"Don't* touch me! Stop *touching* me!"

"Sophia!" She fought me, grabbing at my hands, trying to catch them in her own. "Sophia, stop it!" She managed to snag my wrists and dug her fingers in until I winced and looked at her, tears streaming down my face. "I need your help." Her face was streaked with tear stains, pale pink lines etching a river through the thick red blood on both cheeks. *Where did that come from?*

"With what?" I whispered.

32

"I need you to tell me if you recognize someone." I nodded and Lucy helped me to my feet. I wobbled as she led me away from Jax. Part of me still prayed that this was only a dream, that I was still asleep at the camp and Jax was right beside me, snuggled in her nest of blankets, Mason's tucked safely under her head so she could smell him. Lucy walked me to the other side of the clearing, hauling me along with her. I caught her glancing back at me once or twice, her forehead creased deeply as she looked at me.

"Hello, little mouse." The familiar voice sent jolts of electricity racing down my spine, every nerve ending coming alive as fear slammed down on me. I peered around Lucy and found his cold brown eyes locked on me. I tried to take a step back, struggling to pull my arm free of Lucy's grip but she held on tighter.

She dragged me a few steps closer. "Do you recognize him?" I nodded and she made me turn to face another familiar face. Ice-blue eyes froze me in place, a smile crinkling the scabbed-over twin of my own cut.

"Hello Sophia," Luke purred.

"What about this one?" she asked. I nodded again and she finally released my arm.

I looked between the brothers. Luke lifted his hand to wave at me with his fingers and I stumbled back away from him. I stared at him with wide eyes and his tongue flicked out to lick the blood from the small cut on his lip, a grin spreading across his face as my stomach turned. I looked over at Lucy but she was staring at Christopher as she pulled the sword from its home on her back. She stalked toward him, circling him like a predator closing in on its prey. Christopher tried to keep his eyes on her, following her every move as she closed in. Silver flashed in the sunlight as she struck him, dragging the blade down the length of his arm. He grunted in pain and she swung at him again, catching him in the side.

"You took someone from me," she whispered, crouching so she was eye level with him, staring directly into his face. "Someone important. Why?"

Christopher smiled, blood staining his teeth. "By the time I'm done, you won't have anything left."

Lucy clicked her tongue in a *tsk* sound as she snapped the blade at him, blood weeping from the new wound on his thigh. *"I'm in charge here."* Christopher glared at her and Lucy swung at him again, dragging the blade down his leg, cutting it open from thigh to ankle. "Now, I asked you a question." He cried out and leaned forward, exposing his back for her next blow. This one was deeper than the rest, more blood pouring out and soaking him. "Answer it!" she barked. The smell of pennies burned my nose. I wanted to move away, but I couldn't force myself to. They were finally suffering. *They deserve it.* "We can stop if you just answer the question."

"You bitch!" he spat, pulling at the ropes binding him to the trunk of the tree. She swung the blade again and blood oozed from yet another cut to his back.

"Answer me."

He groaned and leaned to the side, sagging against the rope for the span of a few heartbeats before looking up into Lucy's face. "It felt good to hurt her."

"What did you say?" It was my voice that filled the heavy silence.

"I said it felt good to hurt her," he repeated with a laugh, lifting his face to stare at me. Rage burned inside me, searing me with its heat. *I hate you!* I lurched at him, raking my nails down the length of his face, smiling with sickening delight when I felt his skin come off under my nails, soaking my fingers with the wetness of his blood. He tried to pull away from me, straining at the ropes, as I straddled him, one leg on either side of his thighs, my face inches away from his. I stared into that face, the face of my tormentor, and smiled, my fingers walking up the length of his back, searching for one of Lucy's cuts. My grin grew when I found one and plunged my nails into it, forcing them deep into the skin and muscle.

I laughed when I saw a tear slip down his face. "Big boys don't cry," I taunted, digging my nails in deeper. *I want you to hurt. I want you to suffer.*

"I should have killed you," he growled through clenched teeth.

"Yes," I whispered, leaning closer to his face, "you should have." I found the other cut and sunk my claws into that one, tearing at the skin with all the strength I could manage. I heard Lucy's laugh, a twisted dark sound. When I looked at her, a wicked smile had turned her lips upward and she stalked over to Luke, the blade hanging at her side as she moved. I crawled off of

32

Christopher's lap and kneeled in the blood-soaked grass beside him, my eyes locked on Lucy as she drew closer to Luke.

"I told you that you took something from me," Lucy snarled, "and now, I will take something from you." Christopher's eyes were locked on her as she lifted the sword above her head and brought it down on Luke, blood cascading down the front of him as the tender skin of his throat burst open. A scream that mimicked my own at the loss of Jax burst from him and he lunged forward, straining at the ropes until his wrists were bleeding.

Lucy turned and sauntered back over to Christopher, the blade swinging in her hands. She crouched in front of him, staring directly into his face. "It felt good to hurt him," she whispered.

33

I stared at Christopher in quiet disbelief as tears slipped down his cheeks, his eyes locked on his brother as he bled out. *He deserved worse.* Lucy grinned widely at him as she stood up and wiped the blood from her blade on the sleeve of Christopher's shirt. The adrenaline was still surging through my body and I slowly got to my feet. When I looked at Lucy all I saw was blood. It was dripping from the jagged strands of her hair and soaked into her shirt and jeans in large splotches. Droplets were scattered across her face like crimson freckles, some of them smeared from tears and sweat. Besides our breathing everything was quiet. *Too quiet.*

"Lucy," I whispered. She looked at me and nodded. The birds had gone quiet, the humid morning air too still. The world was holding its breath as predators stalked through the trees. "Jax," I urged.

"Take off your jeans Soph," Lucy said.

"What?" I asked confused, cocking my head.

"The blood."

I looked down at myself, noticing the large blood stains on my knees and shins. I nodded quietly and slipped the rough fabric off, leaving it in a heap beside Christopher. Lucy mimicked me, stripping off her jeans and tossing them beside Christopher. She pulled the hem of her shirt out from her body to look at it, sighed, and slipped it off as well, wiping her face before tossing it over by Luke's now still body.

"Jax," I urged, looking in the direction of our broken angel. She gave me a grim look and bowed her head before turning and heading back to Jax. I followed quietly behind her.

"I'll find you and I'll kill you!" Christopher screamed after us.

Lucy paused and turned her head to look back at him, her face stoic. "You'll never leave this meadow," she said flatly. I didn't look back at him, I didn't care enough to. *Get to Jax. Bring Jax home.*

"Sophia!" he yelled. I froze mid-step. *He's never said your name.* "Luke was so mad! She was just a little girl! I did it as a mercy!" I tried to turn around. I wanted to see if he was lying, but Lucy grabbed my arm.

"Don't look, Soph. He's lying. We've got to hurry." Lucy sighed, looking down at Jax. *She could be sleeping.*

"She looks like a doll," I whispered, leaning down to brush a strand of hair from her cheek, tucking it behind her ear, my fingers lingering on her soft skin. It felt like velvet under my fingertips. I wanted to remember every detail of her and lock it in my mind so I would never forget.

"Sophia," Lucy snapped, grabbing my attention, "we have to get her back to camp." I nodded and Lucy gently nudged me away from Jax with her shoulder, crouching and sliding her hands under Jax's knees and shoulders. With a grunt she lifted her into her arms, staring down at her face. I watched a few tears slip down her cheeks before she turned and began walking back toward camp. I followed along behind her, sneaking only one glance back at the meadow before stepping back into the trees. We were silent as we walked back... I wasn't sure what to say to her. *Your whole world has been taken.*

"Jax!" The hope in Anna-Beth's voice sent a knife through what was left of my heart. A new wave of tears spilled down my cheeks and I desperately searched for Claire's face as I choked on another sob. When I finally met her green gaze she only nodded and reached out to grab Anna-Beth, dragging her back as Lucy and I walked closer. As I stared at Lucy's back, I saw the shaking, her whole body vibrating as she walked. Finally, she stopped and fell to her knees, her arms still clutching Jax's body to her. She bowed her head, laying it lightly on Jax's chest and sobs shook her. I felt my knees buckle and I collapsed beside Lucy, sinking into the sorrow and letting it swallow me.

"What happened?" Claire's voice was soft when she spoke. I glanced up, wiping at my face with the back of my hand. She was right in front of us.

"She's dead," I choked. "They took her."

"Who?" Hope asked, her arms wrapped tightly around a now sobbing Anna-Beth.

"Doesn't matter," Lucy whispered. "They're dead now too."

"What do you want to do with her?" Claire asked gently, reaching her hand out to Jax. Lucy jerked her back, clutching her even tighter to her chest. Claire froze and then pulled her hand back.

"We have to bury her," I whispered.

"We can't," Lucy sobbed. "We don't have time, they'll find us before we're done."

"Who?" Claire asked.

"Shredders," Lucy responded bluntly, lifting her head to look at Claire. "There was a lot of blood when I was done."

Claire nodded and stood back up slowly. "I'll get you two new clothes. We'll figure out what to do with Jax."

"We can't just leave her for those monsters to get," I cried looking at Lucy. She didn't look at me, "We don't have time Soph." *No. You can't leave her.*

"Here you go, sweetheart," Claire whispered, setting a new pair of jeans down in front of me. She laid a shirt and jeans down for Lucy before backing away.

"Flowers," I choked looking up to meet Claire's eyes. "She needs flowers." Claire nodded and walked over to Hope, whispering something to her. Hope nodded and Claire walked toward the patch of wildflowers Jax and Anna-Beth had been picking, Hope and Anna-Beth followed behind her. "I need to grab something," I whispered, struggling to my feet and sliding the jeans from Claire on. Lucy was silent as I walked away, searching for Jax's mound of blankets. The forest green of Mason's blanket drew me to where the girls had slept. I picked the soft blue whale up off Anna-Beth's sleeping bag and held it to my chest, wrapping both arms around it. I buried my face in the stuffed animal, inhaling the scent of Jax that clung to the dingy toy. Fresh tears streaked down my face and I gathered up Mason's blanket, sulking back over to Lucy.

"I don't want to let her go, Soph. I can't do it." She looked up at me, pain consuming her eyes. I knelt down in front of her and laid the blanket and

33

whale down beside me, before reaching out and touching Jax softly.

"I'll help you," I said softly. Lucy nodded and slowly began to lower Jax down, a rainstorm of tears falling and plopping softly on Jax's skin. When she was resting on the ground Lucy pulled her arms out from under her and wrapped them around her exposed torso. I picked up the pile of clothes Claire had left and held them out to her. "You have to get dressed." She took the clothing with a mumbled thank you and began slipping them on. I looked down at Jax and then grabbed Mason's blanket, laying it over her, covering her from chest to toes.

"Here." It was Claire's voice. A small ocean of wildflowers fell beside me and I looked up, smiling weakly at her, grateful for them.

"What are you going to do with them?" Hope asked, laying down another arm full.

"Jax loved flowers, it's only right that she be buried in them." I said grabbing a few. I touched the petals gently, running my fingers against their softness. *Just like the bunny.* I smiled and wiped a stray tear from my cheek before setting the blossoms down. I tucked the edges of Mason's blanket around her, leaving one corner sticking out. "Hope, can I see your knife?" She pulled the blade from the pocket of her sweatshirt and held it out toward me quietly. I took it, the long worn handle smooth in my palm, and began to cut the fabric. I only took enough for the whale. I handed the knife back and laid the fabric beside the whale. I started to finish tucking the blanket under Jax's legs and froze when I saw a strange mark on her ankle. I pushed the torn bits of her pants aside and nearly choked. Indented into her skin were teeth marks, deep enough that they had begun to weep blood. Christopher's words echoed in my head. *I did it as a mercy... he saved her from his brother.*

I finished tucking the blanket around her quickly, trying to banish the thought of Luke's teeth on Jax's skin. My own bites ached at the very thought. I reached and grabbed the fabric and the tattered blue whale from the grass beside me. Slowly, I wound the fabric around it. *Safe.*

"Let us help," Claire said, reaching down and picking up a bunch of the flowers. I nodded and set the whale down, reaching for the pile of flowers. Slowly, we covered Jax's small form in the brightly colored blossoms.

Explosions of pink, purple and yellow adorned her body, bathing her in their beauty. Soon, only her face was exposed.

"I don't want to leave her alone. She doesn't like the dark," I whispered.

"She won't be in the dark," Claire said, touching my shoulder softly. "See all these pine trees?" I nodded. "Fireflies love pine trees. There will be hundreds of 'em out here every night." My chest tightened and I bit back a sob.

"We have to go, Soph," Lucy whispered. I nodded, my eyes still locked on Jax's face, committing every freckle to memory. Claire squeezed me lightly before letting her hand fall away. I glanced behind me as everyone grabbed their bags and slid them on their shoulders.

I turned back to Jax. "Say hello to Mason for us sweet girl," I whispered, pressing my lips to her forehead.

Made in the USA
Columbia, SC
11 November 2024